AMIE

W. M. J. Kreucher

W. M. J. Kreucher
Visit my website at walt.kreucher.net

Printed in the United States of America

First Printing: September 2021

ISBN- 979-8-8693-8127-9

DANDELION MAN
— PRESS —

"It may be said that the chief purpose of life, for any one of us, is to increase according to our capacity our knowledge of God by all the means we have, and to be moved by it to praise and thanks."
— *J. R. R. Tolkien*

*I dedicate this book to my brother-in-law
Terry, who provided the spark of inspiration
for the novel.*

INTRODUCTION

THIS IS THE STORY OF DMITRI Peskov, head of the Russian Federal Security Service, the successor agency to the Soviet Union's KGB. He is the second most powerful man in Russia, reporting directly to the President. Some say he is even more powerful than the President, primarily because he operates in secret and has authority to act necessary in the interest of the State in 'security' matters.

This is also the story of Samuel Kennedy, a mild-mannered American with a penchant for writing computer code. Sam, as he is known to his friends, and Dmitri have never met.

As the story begins, we find Dmitri alone in his apartment, in an affluent residential area in the downtown Presnensky District of Moscow. He is despondent at the loss of his protégé, Vasili Grigoriy Konstantinov, a man whom Dmitri loved as the son he never had.

Dmitri sets out in search of answers that only Sam Kennedy can provide

Chapter 1

Dmitri

WERE I NOT AN AGNOSTIC, I would think I was experiencing the dark night of the soul. I sold my soul many years ago. I can hardly remember having one. I suppose the vodka is taking hold. My doctors warned me about drinking. It affects my heart; they tell me. I haven't got a heart. Not one that can feel anything. Not one that works as it should. I drink more now and enjoy it less. Gone is my wife. Thirty years ago, she left. Dead are my contemporaries. Why does this Christian God spare my life when he has taken everything from me?

Vasili was the only friend I had left in the world. Now, my only friend is darkness. I groomed little Vasili to replace me. He was more than a friend. The son I never had. How I loved it when he called me Uncle Dmitri.

Retirement is not for me. It would be better if I died on a mission like Vasili. How I envy him. But who would avenge my death for the glory of Russia? The Patriks have lost their appeal. The noise of expatriates and their late-night drinking keeps me awake. In the darkness, my thoughts turned to my little Vasili. He was too good at his job to be killed by just any man. Who is this superman who killed my Vasili? There is no American capable of this treachery. Mossad? The devils. They are treacherous enough. Afghanis? They are too stupid. I wonder how they could sneak up on him. Even in his sleep, he would hear anyone coming into his room. I trained him myself.

"If I was not so old, I would avenge Vasili. Now I am good for nothing but drinking. Look, even the Stolichnaya Elit has abandoned me."

The remnants of the bottle dribbled into the glass.

"Another fallen comrade."

The bottle slipped to the floor.

* * *

In the morning, Dmitri finished the drink he had poured the night before. Rising from his chair where he always slept, he stumbled into the kitchen for a piece of black bread and coffee. No longer did he look forward to the day. Not since Vasili Grigoriy Konstantinov had been killed had he been to the office. The very thought of facing his staff, pretending things were normal, gnawed at him. He slammed his fist onto the table, spilling his coffee.

"Why am I sulking like a schoolboy? I must learn who destroyed my dream if it is the last thing I do on this earth."

Dmitri opened the file on the kitchen table and studied each page. He had read the file more times than he could remember. He reread the newspaper accounts of the incident. The New York Times, the Wall Street Journal. They all said the same thing: another cold war is coming and this time the Russians will win.

He chuckled, imagining the drone's flight over Washington and the President cowering in a bunker somewhere below the White House. A tear glistened in the corner of his eye as he read the account of the officer who found the bodies of three individuals in a field in West Virginia. An audible gasp choked his throat as he looked at the photo of the body of Vasili being loaded into the back of an ambulance. Every time he looked at that photograph, it brought a flood of emotion.

Then it struck him. The picture showed only one ambulance at the scene.

"Dmitri, you are getting old. You would not have missed that in your youth."

They would not put three bodies in one truck. He studied the satellite photographs. Military vehicles surrounded the field and the area where the drone crashed. Nowhere did he see another emergency medical vehicle. Fire trucks were on the scene of the crash. Troop transports and military personnel were sweeping the area for debris. He wondered if something fabricated the story to hide the truth.

Dmitri picked up the phone and made a call.

"Yes, Sir." The female voice on the other end responded.

"Roza, I want Unit 26165 to investigate the events leading up to the death of Comrade Konstantinov."

"Yes sir, I will contact Unit 56162 tonight." Roza spoke the number slowly, deliberately.

Dmitri quickly dressed and walked outside towards Barrikadnaya station. He had much to do.

Chapter 2

MANY WOULD CALL MIESHA SOKOLOV a snake in the grass. Not to his face, mind you; but they spoke it in hushed tones in back rooms. Those who opposed him dared not do so publicly. Miesha was the son-in-law of a former president and rose through the ranks on the strength of his political backers and not on his skills or his intellect. Miesha's value to the Federal Security Service of the Russian Federation (FSB) fell after his father-in-law resigned from office. Still, Miesha remained powerful.

With Dmitri Peskov wallowing in self-pity and depression, Miesha saw his opportunity. Miesha hated Vasili Grigoriy Konstantinov for the simple reason that Dmitri loved him. Though he was never told directly, Miesha suspected Vasili would be appointed to head FSB when Dmitri Peskov retired. With Vasili dead and Dmitri out of the picture, Miesha seized command. He instituted a Ministry of Truth. He put his people in positions that would indoctrinate esteemed members of the press to his truth, his way of viewing the world. Anything not approved by the ministry was labeled 'misinformation' and was banned from social media sites. People who opposed him disappeared. Miesha saw Russia and the world as being put there to serve him. In this way, he was the direct opposite of Dmitri. While there was no doubt Dmitri was ruthless in pursuit of his goals; his goals always aligned with the greater good of Mother Russia.

Miesha picked up the phone and dialed. "Katerina, meet me in ten minutes. You know the place." He hung up the phone and lit his cigar. Grabbing his hat from the wooden coat rack that stood behind the door, he flicked off the lights and nodded to Roza as he exited the office.

Katerina Zaytsev was a Russian beauty. At five and a half feet tall, her slender figure made men turn as her silhouette passed beneath the streetlight. Her eyes were not quite gray, but not golden either. They were soft, inviting. A man could get lost in them. She entered the bar and took a seat at the back, facing the front door. The rear exit was a few meters to her right.

Dmitri sat on the edge of the monument that supported the Solovetsky Stone in Lubyanka Square, across from the building where he had worked these past twenty years. He watched the lights in his office turn dark; the garrote wire twisting in his hands.

Miesha Sokolov turned up the collar of his suit coat as protection from the wind as he crossed the street and cut through the square. He was on his way to meet Katerina at Razvedka's. She was to perform a small favor for him. He paid no attention to the old man sitting on the stone.

* * *

"Miesha? Not even a hello for your old friend?" Dmitri expertly slipped the wire garrote around Miesha's neck and wrenched the ends tighter with each word he spoke. "I know about your meeting with 'the widow maker'. She will not leave the bar tonight. You are as predictable as you are stupid. You think you can outsmart an old fox like me by putting your people in place, taking over my office while I work on official State business — commissioning an assassin to — well, let us just say your lack of training has spoiled your plans. I never taught you everything I knew. There was no need. You would never replace me. You bumbling idiot."

The cigar fell from Miesha's mouth as the last gasp of air spilled from his lips. His eyes closed and his body went limp. Dmitri caught him, then propped him on the monument, leaning his body against the Solovetsky Stone. "I never told you I was born in a prison camp. It is fitting that you have come to the end of your life at a memorial to a prison camp. Rest in peace, my friend."

Dmitri unwrapped the wire from Miesha's neck and slipped it into his pocket. Glancing around, he saw no one in the square. He turned toward Razvedka's.

Dmitri felt nothing; not the slightest hint of remorse at the loss of a comrade. He never liked Miesha. He tolerated him but never trusted him.

When Dmitri walked into the bar, a look of surprise flashed in Katerina's soft eyes. The glow of the dim incandescent light above the table made her eyes appear golden. "Comrade Peskov, what a pleasant surprise. It is an honor to see you. Please join me." She motioned to the chair across from her.

Dmitri sat across from the attractive woman. "I have always admired golden haired Russian women. They are the most beautiful women in the world, don't you agree?"

"You flatter me, Comrade." Katerina often heard compliments from men, just never from someone like Dmitri Peskov. She closed her eyes and turned her head slightly. She did not blush.

"The candle flame flickering in your golden eyes invites a man deeper into your soul. But what a fool I am. You are obviously expecting a male companion tonight and I do not wish to interfere. Anton, two glasses and a bottle of Talvarish."

The bartender brought two glasses and a bottle of Russian vodka; the name of the vodka translated to 'comrade'. Anton quickly put the items on the table and left. Dmitri took out his knife, slit the seal, and opened the fresh bottle. He poured two generous servings. He put one in front of Katerina. "Let us drink to our fallen comrades. It is fitting, is it not, to toast with this vodka?"

Katerina nodded, then raised her glass, smiled at Dmitri, kissed the edge of her glass as if it would be her last, then drank. She lowered the empty glass and gently placed it on the table in front of her. She looked at Dmitri, anticipating an explanation.

Dmitri reached across the table and placed his hand on Katerina's. She felt a prick.

"You are wondering if I injected you with Novichok. No, my dear. It is not. It is a new formulation. Our best chemists have been working in secret for years. I am giving you a great honor. You are the first to experience it. As far as we know, there is no antidote. You have but moments to live. Is there anything you wish to tell me?"

"Dmitri, forgive me. Miesha told me you had lost your mind after they killed Vasili. I was just protecting Mother Russia."

"Well, Miesha was correct - to a point. I have become focused on finding those responsible for killing my beloved Vasili. I will not stop until I avenge his death." Dmitri placed his right hand under Katerina's chin and stroked her soft cheek with his thumb. "Goodbye, my dear. I am sorry. We could have been such good friends had you not chosen so poorly."

With that, Dmitri rose, bowed to his comrade across the table, and doffed his hat to Anton on the way out. Slowly, he made his way to the Lubyanka Metro station down the street.

Chapter 3

Dmitri

IN THE MORNING, DMITRI WALKED into the reception area outside his office, whistling a patriotic tune. "Good morning, Roza."

Roza smiled. "Comrades Yuri Koslov and Kliment Alekseev are waiting for you." Her boss seemed chipper as he entered his office for the first time in weeks.

"Excellent, could you tell Comrade Sokolov I need to speak with him about this operation as soon as possible? If he is available, have him join us." Dmitri made the comment loud enough for the two men in his office to overhear.

"Comrade Sokolov has not arrived yet." Roza followed Dmitri into his office.

"That is not like Miesha. The mice have been playing while the cat was away. I will reprimand him for his laziness when I see him." He smiled as he spoke the words.

"Yes, Sir. Will there be anything else?"

"I do not wish to be disturbed." There was no need for Dmitri to acknowledge the coded warning Roza gave the previous day—especially in front of others.

"Understood. I have left the list of personal changes on your desk." Roza winked at her boss as she left the room; being careful, the two men could not see her acknowledgement of the unstated message. She closed the door behind her.

Roza Shanina was married to the job and totally devoted to Uncle Dmitri, as she called him, in their private moments. Her parents named her after her grandmother, a decorated World War II hero. Her grandmother had fought in the famous battle of Vilnius and was the first woman sniper to be awarded the Order of Glory for her fifty-nine kills.

Roza had been with Dmitri Peskov for most of his career at the FSB and advanced in stature as Dmitri rose through the ranks. Though unrequited, she secretly loved Vasili Grigoriy Konstantinov. She wanted to avenge Vasili's death almost as much as Dmitri did.

"Comrades, I am giving you authorization to review Comrade Konstantinov's private files. You will each monitor the other to ensure confidentiality of the information. No one is to know the contents except me. Is that understood?" Dmitri walked over to his desk, took out a sheet of stationery with his letterhead, and began writing.

The two men swallowed hard and looked at each other.

"Find anything that may be of use in tracking down those responsible for his death. And be quick about it."

Koslov and Alekseev rose as Dmitri handed them the signed authorization. They turned and quickly exited the office.

Dmitri walked over to the office window and stood watching the police in the square across the street. They were loading a body into an ambulance.

* * *

Unit 26165, code name SOFACY, worked through the night and the night after that, checking and rechecking the records. Evgeny Naumov, Fancy Bear to his friends, programed the information into the Project Asymmetry computer. This was the first time SOFACY had worked with the artificial intelligence-based Asymmetry computer. It wasn't Fancy Bear's first experience. As a teen, he helped Russia create the dark web, then exploited its potential as a Black Hat hacker. Now, he worked for the State, at least most of the time. He guarded his precious Asymmetry like a mother protects her child. Only on orders from the top would he permit its use for such plebeian tasks as finding people.

Evgeny's skills at finding hidden things and people were legendary. It was he who, in the years before artificial intelligence, had discovered Dmitri Peskov's real identity.

Searching backwards from Dmitri's current position as head of the FSB to his position in the Main Directorate, Evgeny located Dmitri's records at the Higher Intelligence School in the area just north of Chelebityevo, near Moscow, which provides 'special training'. Evgeny then located Dmitri's records at the Second Chief Directorate before they transferred him to the First Chief Directorate. Evgeny uncovered information on the foreigners and consular officials Dmitri had monitored. He located the top-secret file that Dmitri's commander compiled when the Red Army discovered the identity papers Dmitri used to enlist were not real. Rather than expelling him from service, the military command selected him as a candidate for the KGB school in Okhta, Leningrad. Evgeny traced Dmitri through two dozen identities before the time he volunteered for the Red Army as a teenager. Dmitri's story to the Base commander was that he lived as an orphan on the streets of Moscow. The challenge for Evgeny was to uncover the identity of this particular orphan. Using his contacts on the dark web, Evgeny pieced together rumors of children who followed soldiers out of the concentration camps and hid on trains that took them to Moscow.

* * *

Yuri Koslov and Kliment Alekseev were assigned to review Vasili's paper records, all of which were classified as 'particularly important'. Only the highest levels were permitted to review the folders containing his 'assignments'.

The folder covering the details of Vasili's last assignment was brought into the secure reading room. Even then, just two comrades were permitted to read the folder, each one responsible for watching the other.

What the two agents discovered puzzled them. The assignment started oddly. Comrade Konstantinov seemed to be reviewing social media intelligence from overseas during the Brussels operation. There was no record of what started him down the path to America. The two comrades closed the file and put it in the safe. They exited the room and commandeered a desk and a phone.

They placed calls to the Brussels office. Yuri called the Commandant. The call produced no useful information. The Commandant did not know that Comrade Konstantinov was ever in Brussels.

Yuri smiled at his partner, "typical".

Yuri and Klim began calling the technicians. One by one, they meekly answered the phone. After interviewing twenty-four technicians, finally one admitted to talking to Comrade Konstantinov.

"What did he want?" Klim barked, losing patience with the drawn-out interrogation.

"That is difficult to say. The 'tweet' seemed harmless."

"Tweet? What tweet?"

"I can't recall exactly, Comrade Konstantinov told me to delete it immediately and instructed me not to discuss it with anyone."

"I am empowered by the Director of the FSB to receive this information, do you understand?"

"Yes, Comrade Alekseev."

"Then tell me what the message said."

"Something about stealing a drone."

"A drone? One of ours?"

"I do not know."

"And what was the target? Mother Russia?"

"Also, unclear. The message had no specific target. We got a location and the name of the individual who sent the message. Comrade Konstantinov made me erase that information, too."

"And what happened then?"

"Comrade Konstantinov left the room. No one saw him after that."

"You're sure you're telling us all you know?"

"Yes, Sir." The technician's voice quivered.

"Alright."

Klim hung up the phone and turned to his partner.

"Comrade, it seems our friend was investigating a possible terrorist plot. But why would he go to America?"

"You're certain he left Brussels for America?"

"Da. The flight plan was in the folder."

"That is odd. Is it possible the CIA was plotting something against the Motherland? An assassination plot, perhaps?"

"That would explain why he was killed."

"The CIA? But why would they steal one of their own drones, and what or who was the target?"

"You're thinking someone else was involved? A double agent? And the CIA thought our comrade was behind the plot?"

"That is also a possibility."

"Then the CIA was definitely involved?"

"Why else would the military be at the scene so quickly and fabricate such a ridiculous story in the American press?"

"Should we close the investigation?"

The two men looked at each other and shook their heads. They knew from experience that speculation without proof would not be accepted. Not by the head of the FSB.

* * *

It took Fancy Bear forty-eight hours to program his computer. He started by hacking into the FSB mainframe. It was easier and quicker than asking for permission to see the files. On the mainframe were all the details of Vasili Grigoriy Konstantinov's 'black ops'. Evgeny programed Asymmetry to hack into State computers for each of the countries where the ops had occurred and find the files for every assassin, every extraction team, and every agent who might want Vasili dead. Then he fed in all the news reports from Vasili's last trip to the United States and let the computer do its thing.

He spent the next seven days analyzing backup data files from Brussels. Asymmetry evaluated every event, every social media post, every notation in every computer file in the days before Comrade Konstantinov left Brussels. There was no mention of a drone and no mention of a terrorist plot. The rest of the team focused on the events emanating out of Detroit, where Comrade Konstantinov traveled. The search was expanded to encompass the entire metropolitan area. Still, no breakthrough was discovered. Yuri and Kliment broke out in a cold sweat each time the phone rang and their throats tightened when they answered, fearful that it was the Chief demanding an update.

Getting nowhere, they decided to work backwards from the actual incident that led to the death of their fallen comrade. Press reports emanating from every local television and radio station were studied. They compared pictures of the drone flying over Washington to known military aircraft. The team quickly identified the unmanned aerial vehicle as an MQ-9 Reaper manufactured by General Atomics.

"Why would the CIA steal an older model?"

"It's looking more and more like the CIA was not behind this, comrade."

"Da."

"If not them, who?"

"Syria? Iran? North Korea? America has many enemies."

"True, but none that would cause Comrade Konstantinov to get involved. Nothing would make him happier than to watch a terrorist event on American soil."

"We are no closer to the truth than when we started."

Yuri and Klim walked into the office to confer with Evgeny.

"Are you playing Galaga?" Klim asked, incredulous at the images on the monitor.

"I enjoy the classics, besides the search is running in the background." Evgeny minimized the screen; the game dropped from sight and revealed the search engine's progress: eleven percent.

It was on a Monday that Evgeny hacked into the FBI database and identified three names: Ziar el Muhammed, James Patrick O'Connor, and Samuel Kennedy. The report he found showed that the latter two individuals were killed in the field, along with Vasili Konstantinov. Two questions remained. What were they doing in the field and why were their names left off from the newspaper report of the incident?

Chapter 4

Dmitri

THE NEXT DAY, YURI AND KLIMENT were summoned to the Chief's office. Evgeny stayed in the background as he always did.

The pair quietly shuffled in and took their seats at the circular table in the corner of the office. The bullet-proof glass, which covered two entire walls, looked out over Lubyanka Square. From their vantage point in the corner office, they could see the Solovetsky Stone across the street. Dmitri sat at his desk as he finished reading the report. He lifted the small copper cezve and poured the coffee into his cup, then took a sip. He walked over to the table and sat opposite the two men.

"What do you have to tell me?"

"Sir, we have uncovered the names of the two Americans who were killed with Comrade Konstantinov and one other individual who was involved in the operation."

"Well?"

"Samuel Kennedy, James Patrick O'Connor, and Ziar el Muhammed."

"And do we know who these agents work for? Are the names aliases? Do we know their real names?"

"No, Sir. We thought it unimportant since Comrade Konstantinov killed Kennedy and O'Connor. We don't know what happened to Muhammed. Our investigation is still underway."

"Fools. Don't they teach you anything anymore at K1? Do you really think Kennedy and O'Connor are dead? Did you not consider the fact that this is just a cover story?"

The two men stared with wide eyes at each other.

"We ... we considered it, but concluded that Comrade Konstantinov would certainly kill anyone who tried to assassinate him."

Dmitri chuckled. "That part is true. Unless he didn't fear them or he trusted them."

"Comrade Konstantinov trusted no one."

Dmitri nodded, then frowned. "Also, true. And what about the Bulgars?"

"The Bulgars?"

"Yes, you fool. The men Vasili visited in America."

"We have not finished our intelligence gathering on that facet of the operation."

"Well, be quick about it. I suspect that the two Americans, if that is what they are, know more about this than anyone."

"You don't think the two Americans are dead?"

Dmitri pressed two fingers of his left hand against his forehead as if to relieve a tension headache. "Is there no one left in the organization that knows what they are doing? Find these two and that Muhammed character and tell me where they are. I will interrogate them myself."

* * *

Yuri and Kliment left the office.

"Bulgars? There was nothing in the file about Bulgarians?" Yuri quizzed his partner.

"How did Peskov know about the Bulgars, and what did he know?" Klim responded.

21

Yuri shrugged as the two men walked down the hall. "Would you like to go back and ask?"

Klim raised his eyebrows, surprised that his partner would even raise that option. He shook his head. The pair proceeded directly to Evgeny's cubbyhole in the basement of the Lubyanka Building. The setting suited his personality. Cold and dank.

"We need to focus on finding two Americans, Kennedy and O'Connor and some foreigner, Ziar el Muhammed. And what can that stupid computer tell us about the Bulgars that Comrade Konstantinov contacted in America?" Kliment shouted.

Evgeny's eyebrows shot up and his eyes widened. It wasn't often that anyone dared raise their voice at him. He knew too much. No secret was safe from his prying. He had ways to hurt your career without you even knowing. "The boss didn't like what you told him?"

"He is impatient. We all knew that. And now that his little protegee is lost, he is obsessed. He demands answers, not speculation." Yuri chimed in. His softer tone seemed to appease Evgeny, who had already started coding a search on Koslov and Alekseev.

"You know that the boss and Vasili were both orphans that grew up on the streets."

Yuri's and Klim's eyes widened as they looked at each other, then back at Evgeny.

"What? You didn't think I would be interested in my boss's history? Perhaps you are correct. A slight diversion down a rabbit hole searching for American aliases might be fun." Evgeny loved a challenge. He coded in the search parameters.

When the two agents left, Evgeny got up from his workstation and walked over to the rows of processors lined against the entire back wall. He tenderly patted the side, soothing his beloved. "They didn't mean what they said about you. We can forget about it—this time."

Chapter 5

Niklas aka Dmitri

IMPATIENT WITH THE PACE OF THE NEW, technology-based techniques. The next day, Dmitri left Moscow for Washington, DC. He was 'old school', preferring tried-and-true techniques. He traveled under an alias, one he hadn't used since the Cold War ended, Niklas Sussman.

Niklas traveled on a tourist visa that he had issued himself. His cover was that of a retired oligarch, a senior vice president with Lukoil, who had a penchant for the decadent life of the American oil executives about whom he had heard so much. He chose the rank to be high enough to be important, yet not so high that he would be known internationally. Dmitri spoke freely on the flight with passengers and crew alike and came across as chatty, the friendly old uncle that everyone loves to invite to dinner.

Dmitri, or rather Niklas, arranged for an extended stay at the Embassy Circle Guest House on R Street in NW Washington, DC. The location was idyllic, just five minutes from the Russian Embassy; seven minutes from the Ambassador's residence, and around the corner from Woodrow Wilson's house.

The first night, Niklas dined with two Americans he met on the plane. His goal was to establish an identity as a tourist interested in American culture. The next morning, he toured Wilson House, on a high hill commanding an extensive view of the Potomac. They filled the home of the former president with memorabilia and it remained decorated much as it had when Wilson lived there with his wife, Edith, after his term ended. As he walked through the artifacts, Niklas recalled how, at the end of World War I, the treacherous Americans, under orders from Wilson, invaded the Motherland to steal what they could while the Red Army lay in tatters.

The following day, Niklas toured the Smithsonian, walked the Mall, and circled the Tidal Basin. He stopped at the World War II memorial, where he sat on a stone bench and reflected on his parents, trying to imagine what they were like. Dmitri remembered little of them. Faded images, more emotion than fact.

* * *

The year was 1941, almost two years after Germany signed a non-aggression pact with the Russians and a year after Germany began planning to break the treaty. The war had taken its toll on German men, machinery, and natural resources. Russia had plenty to spare. The German High Command coveted the oil reserves of the Caucasus and the rich cropland that would provide much needed food for the troops and the German people.

A young, lean lieutenant on his first leave from the Polish front approached the raven-haired woman sitting alone at the table in a dark corner of the restaurant.

"May I join you?" Lieutenant Vladimir Kovalev said as he pulled out the wooden chair.

"Suit yourself. It's still a free country and we honor our military men." The moderately attractive Commissar, Lyudmila Abramovich, never looked up from her papers.

"I am Lieutenant Vladimir Kovalev, at your service." He clicked the heels of his black boots before sitting down. The black military uniform he wore suited him, made him more distinguished.

Vlad motioned for the waitress to bring him a vodka and another drink for the lady. "With your permission."

Lyudmila nodded. She finished the page she was reading, then reached out her hand. "I am Commissar Abramovich. How does the fighting go?"

Vladimir made a fine soldier, tall and handsome. His intellect allowed him to advance in rank. But his charisma caused the troops to follow him with blind fidelity. The same charisma gave him the confidence to approach any woman, even one who carried herself with such grace as to command the attention of an entire brigade. "The Russian troops fight gallantly. It will be a matter of days before we repel the treacherous Germans."

Commissar Lyudmila knew better. She knew firsthand the war did not go well. Her political abilities were highly desired, but it was her training as a sharpshooter that made her invaluable in Brest, near the Polish border.

Vladimir took notice of Lyudmila. Not so much for her physical beauty, but there was something about her that commanded his attention. She was the perfect Political Commissar—the go—between connecting the military to the civilian government. Mother Russia did not want generals running things.

During the day, Lyudmila interfaced with the military leaders and reported back to her superiors. In the evening, she took up her sniper position in the Church steeple, guarding against incursions.

Sleep during war was always optional. Tonight was a rare chance for Lyudmila to relax before taking up her evening station. Male companionship became a welcome relief from the horrors she saw daily.

"Tell me, do you live here?" Vladimir inquired.

"No, I'm stationed here temporarily—a transient, really—I have no home." Lyudmila never disclosed much about her job—it didn't pay—what with spies everywhere. Yet, Vladimir didn't look like a spy—his features—especially his deep greenish-gray eyes spoke Russian. Those eyes captured her from the instant her eyes met his.

Vladimir and Lyudmila spent their first night together in the church steeple. The close quarters made for a cozy encounter.

Vladimir came back each leave and eventually got permission to take a war-bride. He never told his supervisor the name, always referring to her as Lyubimaya, my beloved.

During war—women dealt with inconvenient pregnancies swiftly— Lyudmila could not bear to part with her unborn child, especially after she received word that Vladimir had been captured and taken to Majdanek. It wasn't long after that incident that the entire town was overrun with German soldiers. The locals quickly pointed out all the Russians and Lyudmila found herself in the same concentration camp. Her husband, Vladimir, never knew. His execution occurred in the early morning hours before Lyudmila arrived.

Lyudmila's child, a boy, was born in the camp. No record acknowledged the birth and few children made it out of the camp.

A local woman, who had lost her child, worked in the camp as secretary to the Commandant. She snatched the boy from his mother's arms before reporting Lyudmila as the Political Commissar. The execution took place before sunset that very day. Lyudmila's eyes closed for the last time at the sight of another woman clutching her baby boy.

* * *

Though he had no memory of his parents, the memory of his early years brought a tear to Dmitri's eye. Gone was any recollection of a woman caring for him in the camp. His only memory was of following soldiers to a train station after the camp was liberated. Not since those days on the streets had he felt so alone.

As he sat on the bench, a man approached.

"May I join you?"

Dmitri nodded.

Though the two had never met, there were no code words exchanged, no secret handshakes. Dmitri's countenance told the man everything he needed to know. Dmitri hadn't ventured outside the motherland in decades. Not because he didn't have friends in America or elsewhere, but because for every friend there were a thousand standing ready to take down the great Dmitri Peskov.

"I am at your command, Comrade."

"I need you to direct some resources. I am looking for those responsible for killing Vasili Konstantinov."

"Da, terrible tragedy. He will be difficult to replace."

"Impossible."

The man nodded in agreement.

"What is it you want me to do?"

"I require answers."

"Of course. Then our comrade was on an official mission?"

"That information is need to know. I want to learn of those responsible for his death."

"I will see to it at once. How can I get in touch with you?"

"Leave your mark on this bench. I will meet you the following day at one o'clock behind the Michigan pillar."

The man got up and left. He had much to do.

Dmitri remained on his bench. He watched people stroll past the memorial, viewing the field of stars. As he got up to leave, he walked over to the North Balustrade, the memorial to the Atlantic Front, and viewed the bas-relief sculpture panels. The pictures depicted the lend-lease program, war bond drives, women in the military, Rosie the riveter, the Battle of the Atlantic, the air war, and the pivotal role of the B-17 and the P-51 Mustang, paratroopers, Normandy, the critical role of tanks and medics, the Battle of the Bulge. Dmitri's focus was on the final panel depicting Russians meeting the Americans at the Elbe River. Germany surrendered twelve days after the events depicted in the sculpture.

How far our relationship has transitioned since that day, Dmitri thought.

Chapter 6

Dmitri

IN THE DAYS THAT FOLLOWED, Dmitri contacted former colleagues and met with them privately at various monuments and tourist areas scattered throughout the District.

Dmitri contacted a woman he knew only as Xiu Juan from the Chinese Ministry of State Security. Having cut his teeth during the 1960s on the politics of the era, Dmitri never trusted the Chinese. He could not forgive Mao Zedong for criticizing Khrushchev over abstract Marxist doctrines. The disputes between the two leaders foreshadowed a larger political battle over which brand of communism would provide the template for the rest of the world.

China had a formidable cyber activity, second only to that of Russia. They could steal the drone. Why they would do so and why Vasili would care was a mystery.

Xiu Juan happily agreed to meet with Dmitri. Doing a favor for Comrade Peskov would mean that he would owe her a favor, and that was a pearl of incalculable price.

Xiu Juan met Dmitri at the National Mall just below the Jefferson Memorial. She looked across the Tidal Basin, admiring the cherry trees as he approached.

"It has been a long time." Dmitri did not smile.

"I need not ask what you seek."

"Then you have information?"

"You know of the Bulgarians?"

"Something. Dirty people. Vasili mentioned a meeting."

"Your friend contacted them. Perhaps it was the last call he made."

"You monitor Russian calls?" Dmitri scowled as he studied Xiu's face for signs of deception.

"No. We have an agreement. You do not monitor us and we do not monitor you."

"Of course." Dmitri nodded. He knew both sides had cheated on the agreement.

"We were monitoring the Bulgarians at a place called Mehanata. It is a restaurant that fronts for illegal activity in New York."

"Did you learn anything?"

"Your man said 'release them'".

"Release who?"

"We don't know. All we learned was that two 'guests' were to be taken to the Central Park North subway station."

"And about the drone?"

"We knew about it even before the Americans. We tried to commandeer it once it had been hijacked but were unsuccessful. The team who stole it is clever. They put measures in place that we have not encountered before or since."

"Who are they?"

"We suspect Mossad, but can't be certain. They are treacherous. Why would one of your people work with them?"

"Why indeed?" Dmitri scratched his chin.

"That is all I can tell you. I will not ask what your man was doing in America. It is a shame that he died in the crash. Terrible accident."

Dmitri did not respond. His lips tightened and a stern look washed over his face.

Xiu Juan took that as her signal it was time to leave.

"I hope you find what you are looking for."

"Thank you. I will repay this kindness someday."

Xiu Juan smiled as she walked towards the Potomac and disappeared into the crowd on the walkway leading towards the Roosevelt Memorial.

Mossad? That hardly seemed possible, thought Dmitri. But then sometimes necessity makes strange bedfellows.

That afternoon, Dmitri met a man known to him as Dong. They met on Jefferson Drive SW outside the National Air and Space Museum under the shade of the trees lining the street. Dong was a skittish man. He was not used to meetings with high-ranking officials. His hands shook as he lit a cigarette when he saw Dmitri coming in his direction.

Dmitri's approach to the North Koreans differed from his approach with the Chinese. He viewed them more like an older brother views a younger sibling. A sibling that needs to be nurtured, protected, instructed in the ways of the world. Dmitri knew North Korea had a burgeoning hacking operation conducted partly with the Chinese.

"Here, let me light that for you." Dmitri pulled out his lighter and lit the cigarette for the Korean. "I trust that you have been told what I am after?"

Dong nodded and exhaled smoke, careful to direct it away from Dmitri.

"What can you tell me?"

"The Democratic People's Republic of Korea does not monitor Russians. We are allies."

"Yes, of course." Dmitri did his best to smile in order to reassure his new friend.

"I am instructed to convey our regrets at the loss of your comrade."

"Thank you." Dmitri grew impatient with all the diplomacy. He wanted answers, not Asian politeness.

"We were not responsible for stealing the drone. We did, however, monitor the site of the crash and observed three bodies being taken from the site."

"Three? Did you witness this personally?"

"No, I sent a comrade who interviewed an eyewitness, a military man with a penchant for Asian women." Dong gave Dmitri a wink.

"Thank you." Dmitri walked away. He had learned all he could from the North Korean.

The final meeting that day was with a man named Prasanna at the Tomb of the Unknown Soldier in Arlington. Prasanna waited for his contact in the seats in front of the Memorial Amphitheater, observing the precision of the military guard.

The relationship between India and Russia reflected Dmitri's views of his contact. The two countries had longstanding strategic, military, and economic partnerships that grew into a mutual respect between the two nuclear powers.

"Did you know the soldiers take twenty-one steps, stop, turn and face the tomb for twenty-one seconds then turn to face back down the mat, change the weapon to the outside shoulder, the shoulder closest to the visitors, to signify that the sentinels stand between the Tomb and any threat. They wait twenty-one seconds, then take another twenty-one steps down the mat?"

Prasanna jumped as the man spoke to him over his shoulder. Though he was of Indian extraction, he did not wear a turban.

"My apologies. I didn't mean to startle you." Dmitri moved into the seat beside Prasanna.

Prasanna pulled out a cigarette and Dmitri lit it for him, then placed the lighter back in his pocket, making sure the man saw the logo.

"I am afraid we have limited information for you. Our intelligence leads us to conclude that the people who killed your asset were hired mercenaries."

"From where?"

"No one knows. We don't know where they came from or where they went."

"But they are alive?"

"We are not aware of any evidence that they were killed. At least not yet." The grin on Prasanna's face seemed to show he knew what Dmitri really wanted.

Dmitri patted the man on the shoulder and got up to leave. That last part was what he had hoped to hear, even if the details were nonexistent.

Dmitri believed the man because he wanted to be the one to kill those responsible for the death of his beloved Vasili.

Chapter 7

Dmitri

THE FIRST THING THE NEXT MORNING, Dmitri used a back channel to contact his old friend John at the Central Intelligence Agency.

"I was wondering when I would hear from you. We have been monitoring you since you arrived."

John and Dmitri had a relationship that spanned many years, predating John's previous position as Acting Director of the National Counterterrorism Center. Now that he was head of the CIA, the closeness of their relationship had proven useful on more than one occasion.

"I had some people I needed to visit. I will retire soon and I wanted to say goodbye in person."

"Meet me at the National Arboretum." John knew from experience that all calls were monitored. He said only what was essential.

* * *

When Dmitri arrived, John was waiting for him. John had left his driver at the entrance and walked to the reflecting pond near the Capital

Columns and sat on the Martin bench. As Dmitri approached, John rose and stuck out his hand. Dmitri brushed it aside and gave John a hug.

"It has been far too long, my friend. What's this nonsense about you retiring?" John couldn't help but notice the sadness in Dmitri's eyes.

"Age overtakes the best of us, I'm afraid." Dmitri shrugged.

"Things won't be the same without you."

"I know what you mean. I don't have the name of my replacement for you."

"No one can replace you."

Dmitri smiled a sad smile. The man who was to replace him was dead.

"So, this is a courtesy call?"

"Partly. I also have a question that you are uniquely qualified to answer."

"Go on."

"The drone incident. What can you tell me from your side?"

A puzzled look crossed John's face.

"We had nothing to do with the theft. My man tracked the perpetrators and tried to stop them. He gave his life to save your country from a terrorist attack." Dmitri did not flinch as he responded to John's look of surprise.

"He should have contacted us. We would have handled it. He caused a lot of headaches for me trying to figure out why your country would do such a thing."

"I apologize. That was not our intent. We didn't have time to contact you. In these things, there are so many dead ends. No one can follow them all. We did not want to trouble you chasing rabbits."

"No, I suppose not. I am sorry for your loss. We don't know much more than you. Everything is counterintuitive. I was there with the President when he was briefed on the incident. Not much in the way of information. Our initial assessment was that you were responsible."

"I can assure you; nothing could be farther from the truth. You have my word on that."

"I am relieved to hear that. It takes a lot of pressure off the current situation."

"Then you know nothing more?" Dmitri asked.

"I'll see what I can find out. FBI took the lead on this one. They called me in to investigate your side. I turned up an empty sack."

"Because we had nothing to do with it."

"I am grateful my men missed nothing. Meet me here in three days and I will provide what I can." John shook Dmitri's hand and walked towards the entrance to the Arboretum. Dmitri strolled through the azalea gardens and the paths lined with cherry trees for an hour before returning to the Guest House, where he stayed.

Chapter 8

The FBI

THE NEXT MORNING, John pulled the Director of the FBI aside as the two men left the morning briefing in the West Wing.

"Jim, I have a favor to ask." John had to look up, as James was exceedingly tall.

"What do you want?"

John pushed James against the wall, and the two men spoke in hushed tones.

"I'm following up on the drone incident and I need access to your 302s."

James looked with suspicion at John.

"I have been doing some investigating overseas and I want to be sure we're not wasting time searching for things you have already looked into. It would save me a considerable amount of manpower if I could rule out certain things."

"I'll see what I can do."

* * *

James met with his deputy director for lunch that afternoon.

"Andy? I had a strange conversation with JB after our morning intelligence briefing. He was asking about Operation Red Rover."

"What could he possibly want to know about that?"

James shrugged his broad shoulders. "Don't know. Anything in the file that might interest him?"

"It's been a while since we closed that case. I can't recall anything that would interest the CIA. I'll look into it and report back. I seem to recall it involved the kidnapping of a couple of women. You know, I may be confusing two cases. I'd better pull the file. Can I get with you tomorrow on this?"

"Fine with me. I didn't sense any urgency. Perhaps it's just idle curiosity."

* * *

After lunch, Andy went back to his office.

"Jean, can you call the records room and have them pull the Red Rover file? I would like to refresh my memory on the conclusions."

"Right away, Sir."

Jean was what you would call competent. Short, dark hair, with a pleasant shape and a cheerful disposition. She was a delight to have in the office.

It didn't take long for the file to appear on Andy's desk. The thin folder was not what he expected. He opened the folder and there were only three 302s. One for the interview with Ziar el Muhammad, one with James Patrick O'Connor, and the other for a Samuel James Kennedy. All the draft copies had already been destroyed. Andrew turned to the last page of the reports and located the names of the agents that conducted the interviews, Cooper and Patton.

At lunch the next day, Andy confided to James. "I didn't find much. Agents Cooper and Patton from the cyber division conducted the interviews. The operation began with the breach of NASA computers. We initially thought the Chinese were behind it, probing for weaknesses in our security. We were uncertain just what they got. It wasn't until we discovered a drone was missing that we investigated. Do you think John wants to look into the hacking?"

"Maybe." James didn't look convinced.

"What is your assessment of the agents doing the interviews?"

"Cooper and Patton? Good men, thorough, not likely to miss anything. Why?"

"Just thinking. Trying to understand what John was after. He had to know about the hacking. He's after something else."

"What?"

"I'm not sure. Any issues with giving him a copy of the folder?"

"Not that I foresee. There's not much in the file that could be of use to the CIA."

"Better ask Cooper and Patton. On second thought, let's keep this close. If something is up, we'd be better served if there are fewer sources of leaks."

"Roger."

Andy noticed the look of concern on James' face, as if his boss was deep in thought. He strode out of the office, walking over the blue FBI logo woven into the gold area rug in the center of the room. Most agents avoided walking over the emblem. Andy was not one of them.

Chapter 9

CIA

JAMES WAS STILL TROUBLED ABOUT what John was after when he pulled him aside after the morning White House intel briefing.

"I have something for you."

"The file I asked for?"

"It's pretty thin. Our people interviewed only three people: Ziar el Muhammad, James O'Connor and Samuel Kennedy."

"Any known terrorist connections?"

"None that our agents uncovered."

"And who are these men?"

"Ziar is the man who owned the computer used to hack into NASA. He claims he sold it to some chisel-faced Caucasian."

"Do you believe him?"

"No, but we didn't have enough evidence to recommend prosecution."

"And O'Connor?"

"A biologist. Kept his nose clean. No previous record. Nothing to suggest he was a troublemaker. Seems his significant other was kidnapped. He claimed he was working to free her."

"Why didn't he notify you?"

"They brought us in on the kidnapping. We didn't connect the dots until the end."

"And Kennedy?"

"Same story. No priors, nothing to indicate a problem. The odd thing was, someone also kidnapped his wife. We investigated that as an isolated incident. O'Connor and Kennedy dropped out of sight and we initially suspected they were behind the kidnappings. It's usually someone close to the case."

"What's Kennedy's occupation?"

"Did freelance work. computer apps, that sort of thing. Nothing sophisticated, mostly productivity tools."

"You think he was behind the hack?"

"Uncertain. Nothing in his history suggests anything remotely like that."

"But he could have if pressed by an outside agent who kidnapped his wife?"

"Possible. It would take a man of unique skills to bypass the encryption on the NASA server."

"Did you follow-up on the hack?"

"Dead end. Whoever was behind the hack covered their tracks."

"A foreign government?"

"Likely, but we can't say that with any certainty. No patterns resembling anything we have seen before or since."

"Thanks, James. Not sure what to make of this, but thanks anyway." Turning away, John scratched his chin as he walked down the hall in the West Wing.

* * *

The following day, at precisely one o'clock, John strolled around the Capital Columns in the Arboretum and sat on the wooden bench named for Richard W. Grefe'. Dmitri walked up from the other side and sat next to him.

"My friend, I need you to tell me again your country had nothing to do with the hacking of NASA."

"None of my people were involved. I know this because I didn't give the order and no one ever defies me, at least not more than once." Dmitri smiled. His mind flashed on Vasili's face as he thought, *perhaps there was one who would do this.*

"We suspect a foreign government hacked into a government server and stole some computer code. The hacker used techniques we have not seen before or since. Whoever was behind the data breach had a level of sophistication beyond our capabilities."

Dmitri nodded. "There are a few nations that have those capabilities."

"Yes. We are aware of that. But ... never mind. I take you at your word that this wasn't a Russian operation."

"Thank you."

"We will be investigating further and eventually we'll discover which nation was behind the attack."

"If I can be of assistance, I can authorize any aid you may require. Tell me, what else have you learned?"

"Only three people were interviewed. Ziar el Muhammad, James O'Connor, and a Samuel Kennedy. O'Connor is a biologist and unlikely to possess sufficient computer skills. The other two are possibilities. Muhammad is the most likely. He has loose connections to known terrorist organizations. We uncovered nothing concrete. We know he owned the computer involved in the hack."

"Thank you, my friend. Perhaps one day I can repay the favor."

Dmitri got up and walked away, taking a circuitous route that led him through the heart of the arboretum. He had much thinking to do.

Chapter 10

Dmitri

DMITRI PULLED OUT HIS CELL PHONE as he walked, opened the app for the FSB, and searched for Ziar el Muhammad. Though his own people had first given him the names, having the information confirmed by an outside source provided assurance he was on the right track. Dmitri texted Evgeny Naumov and requested that he perform a search.

"My friend, I will not presume to tell you your business, but you are authorized to search the FSB files, Yandex or whatever internet search site you people use nowadays. And search those social media sites. Look for Ziar el Muhammad, he is a possible Middle East 'freedom fighter'. And we now know that James O'Connor is a biologist and Samuel Kennedy works with computers. All three were involved in the Konstantinov incident in the United States."

* * *

In the morning, Dmitri contacted the members of Unit 26165 and gave them the same information he provided to Evgeny the day before.

Within a week, dossiers were prepared on all three individuals. In actuality, hundreds of dossiers were prepared, one for each person who matched one of the names. There were shady characters, those with impeccable reputations, and those who fell somewhere between the two extremes. Encrypted copies of the dossiers were sent to Dmitri's laptop.

Dmitri spent days studying the files. At first, he concentrated on Muhammad. Several incidents appeared linked to Muhammad's name. The file descriptions seemed to match many individuals, some of whom were dead. He ordered Unit 26165 to send him copies of all the travel plans from the past twenty years for each Ziar. Included in the files were trips to the Middle East that posed potential issues of a potential involvement with organizations hostile to the United States and some with hostilities towards Russia. One by one, the FSB began assigning priorities to the personas behind the names.

"Why would this freedom fighter get involved with Vasili? Why would Vasili try to stop him?" Dmitri thought out loud. None of this made any sense to him. "What was the connection?"

Chapter 11

Dmitri

THE JUMBLE OF DOSSIERS began taking its toll. Dmitri ate little and slept even less as he studied and restudied the information in front of him. He needed to find a shortcut through the stack of papers. He tagged his friend in the CIA in the usual way and they met the following day at the arboretum.

"John, I want to know who killed my asset."

"You're not thinking of vengeance, are you?"

Dmitri did not answer.

"You needn't bother. He's already dead."

Dmitri's brow furrowed.

"It's true." John pulled out a photograph of three bodies lying in a field, each covered with a cloth.

"All those involved are dead. Your man shot the others, one of whom somehow managed to kill your asset. We're not sure which one. I don't suppose it matters now. We put all three men in the same ambulance and took them to the morgue."

Dmitri only nodded.

John got up and walked away, leaving the picture in Dmitri's hands. As he left, he turned his head over his shoulder and said, "I hope this puts an end to your search, my friend."

Dmitri tightened his lip but did not answer. The conversation left him puzzled. Why would the photograph show three bodies? If the men who killed Vasili were dead, why did the Americans interview three other individuals? What did these three men know?

The sky darkened as storm clouds gathered over the District. On his way out of the Arboretum, Dmitri paused and sat on a bench looking at the entrance. It was as if his will to move had somehow vaporized under the pressure of retribution. He watched as patrons stopped at a food truck and purchased hot dogs. A tear glistened in the corner of his eye at the sight of children eating ice cream cones. He shook his head, trying to dispel the darkness. "What is the connection? Why can't I see it?" he whispered to no one in particular. Sheets of rain swept across the grounds; the wind blew debris through the parking lot. The other guests who came to the Arb for a peaceful afternoon began scurrying towards their cars. Even then, Dmitri could not bring himself to get up from the bench or even turn his collar against the forces of nature.

Chapter 12

FBI

THE FSB SEARCH ON SOCIAL MEDIA triggered alerts in the counter-intelligence unit of the FBI. Several individuals were assigned the task of determining why Russia would be interested in these people.

The number of people conducting searches for the three names increased to where the names began popping up on Google and Bing searches as top 'hits'.

Trouble was, no one doing the searches, not even Fancy Bear, knew what or who they were looking for. Nothing seemed to raise any eyebrows in the intelligence community.

* * *

Because the 'Red Rover' incident had been kept Top Secret, few in the FBI ranks knew the details. NSA was contacted and asked to monitor any activity from foreign sources that mentioned any of the three names.

Wiretaps were sought and obtained from the Foreign Intelligence Surveillance Court. Within the FBI, the investigation brought little attention. No one cared what was going on because, as far as anyone could tell, no crime had been committed—yet.

The first hint of a possible thread that could lead somewhere came in a casual conversation about Ziar. Two Iranian Quds operatives, the branch of the Islamic Revolutionary Guard specializing in unconventional warfare and military intelligence operations, were overheard discussing Ziar's involvement in the drone terrorist attack, "the defensive warfare perpetrated on the capital of the 'Iblis' is no doubt the work of a Salafi jihadist," was all the message conveyed.

That tip led investigators within the NSA to focus on names associated with the terrorist activity in Washington, DC.

Consultations between NSA and the FBI sharpened the scope of the investigation as to what the Russians were searching for. Finally, they had something they could sink their teeth into.

Chapter 13

FBI

THE FIRST HINT THAT THE FOCUS of the investigation had shifted to terrorist activity brought a stir of excitement within the Bureau. It became the talk of the watercooler and everyone wanted to be in on stopping the next terrorist action.

Eventually the 'Records Keeper' heard the watercooler talk. He instantly recognized the significance of the request to review the Red Rover documents he had received some weeks back. The 'Records Keeper' called Agent Cooper.

"Coop? Don't ask who this is."

Agent Cooper's eyes widened as he stared across the desk at his partner, motioning with his head for Patton to pick up the extension.

"I received a call about the Red Rover operation. Can't tell you who placed the document request, but it was the highest level. Now there is international chatter searching for the names mentioned in the 302s. Thought you should know."

An audible click followed the last word.

Cooper looked at Patton, who shrugged his shoulders.

"What could management possibly want?"

"Beats me. Think we missed something?"

"I doubt it. The story from O'Connor and Kennedy checked out down to the last 't' being crossed. Sure, there were holes in the 'Ziar' relationship with Hamas, but that was all ancillary to the drone incident. Kennedy confirmed he was the one behind the hack and that someone else dumped the computer in order to send us down a blind alley."

"We didn't include that part in the 302s, did we?"

Cooper shook his head. "Didn't want to red flag anyone unnecessarily."

"Think we should notify O'Connor and Kennedy?"

"And tell them what? Or are you suggesting Kennedy wasn't being truthful?"

Agent Patton shrugged his shoulders. "We need to find out what's going on."

Chapter 14

AGENT JOHN COOPER WAS AN AFFABLE MAN, the kind people gravitated towards. He loved to socialize and be around other people. On most days, when he wasn't sitting at his desk or tracking down a lead, he could be found at the watercooler.

"Bill, what's the latest skinny?" Agent Cooper asked, reaching for a paper cup and filling it with water before handing it to his colleague.

"My contact at the CIA told me that FSB was searching social media sites for would-be terrorists in the US."

"Here? Why would the Russians be searching for terrorists here? Do they think Americans would attack Russia?"

"That's the odd thing. They aren't searching the normal terrorist sites or even the dark web. They seem to be searching for someone hiding in plain sight."

"Any common threads?"

"Yes—and no—they're searching for a jihadist named Ziar, something or other. The other two names are as American as yours or mine."

"Really?"

"Yeah, Kennedy and O'Connor."

Agent Cooper nearly spit out the water he had just sipped. He dropped his paper cup into the trash bin. "I gotta go—just remembered I'm supposed to be meeting Patton about a case."

Cooper turned and practically ran back to his office.

"Jim, we've got a problem. Remember the Red Rover case?"

"Sure—we were talking about it the other day, odd case. No charges. A couple of kidnappings. The kidnapper died in an accident involving a stolen drone."

Agent Cooper thought back to the call from the record keeper. "Remember the call we got? Turns out that the Russian FSB is behind the searches. They have the names of all three individuals we interviewed."

Agent Patton's eyes widened. "How? Why? You don't think?"

Agent Cooper shrugged. "Don't know. Did we miss something? You don't think the Russians are out for retribution, do you?"

"More to the point, should we connect with ..."

Before Patton could finish, Cooper interrupted, "Absolutely. But we need to keep this on the DL. No telling how the names leaked, but they had to come from inside the Bureau. The call we received the other day about the document request must have..."

Coop nodded and went to the file cabinet. He looked up the contact information for Kennedy, O'Connor, and Ziar. He got a secure line, then dialed the first name.

"Mr. Kennedy, this is Agent Cooper from the FBI. We spoke with you awhile back regarding the kidnapping of your wife."

"Yes sir, I recall. Can I help you with something?"

"I wanted to relay some information. But first, I need to ask you a question. Are you writing any more apps?"

Kennedy was silent for a moment. The question brought back bitter memories. "No. I got out of that business. Why do you ask?"

"In the past few weeks, several individuals associated with Russian intelligence have begun social media and internet searches for you, Mr. O'Connor, and Mr. Muhammed."

"Pat? What do they want with us? Don't tell me. They found out we were behind the killing of a Russian."

"Seems so. As far as we can tell, they have not narrowed their search down to you specifically. Fortunately, you have a common name. At some point in the not-too-distant future, we are concerned that they will find your current information."

"What could they do to us on US soil?"

"The Russians are fond of using Novichok, a fast-acting nerve agent, to poison enemies of the state. It's easy to smuggle into the country."

Sam nearly dropped the phone.

An audible gasp could be heard on the other end. "Mr. Kennedy. I understand your concern. We will do everything in our power to keep you safe. We are prepared to put you into a Witness Protection program and relocate you and your wife."

"That would mean I would have to cut off all contact with my current life."

"Afraid so. Until we find out exactly what their intentions are, the Bureau thinks this is the best course of action."

"Have you spoken with Pat yet?"

"Agent Patton is trying to get him on the phone now in order to relay the same information. We suggest the two of you refrain from any direct communication just to be on the safe side."

"Understood. Can I talk this over with my wife and get back to you?"

"Of course. This is a big decision. I would advise you to stay off social media and the internet for the time being. No telling what keywords would trigger a 'hit' by the Russians."

"A hit? As in assassination?"

"Sorry, slip of the tongue. I meant a recognition of a keyword that would lead the Russians to you."

"One is as bad as the other."

* * *

Sam felt his heart pounding in his chest at an ever-increasing rate. His legs tingled, preventing him from moving as he hung up the phone. He reached for a chair and sat for what seemed like an eternity. *What am*

I going to do? He thought. *How can I protect Helen?* He couldn't bear the thought of losing the girl he had known since kindergarten.

Sam shook his hands, attempting to release the tension. He got up, grabbed his coat, and proceeded out the door. Perhaps a walk would clear the cobwebs. He had to make a plan, and he needed to do it quickly.

Chapter 15

THERE WERE NOW THREE Russian teams searching for the individuals responsible for killing Vasili. The Russia-based team of agents began tracing Vasili's steps from the time he left Brussels. Fancy Bear did the same with his computer program, feeding it with more parameters as facts and speculation unfolded. Dmitri led the third team in the US.

It didn't take long to identify the Bulgars Vasili had contacted.

Yuri Kozlov notified Dmitri.

"Sir, we have an update."

"What have you to tell me, Yuri?"

"It seems there is a place, Mehanata's in New York, where our friend visited. We can confirm that he visited the establishment once and called a phone in the vicinity a couple of times."

"Thank you. I will take it from here."

Dmitri hung up the phone. Now his own people had confirmed the information he heard in his conversation with Xiu Juan from the Chinese Ministry of State Security. He placed a call to the head of the Bulgarian Intelligence Agency. They provided a name, Natasha, and a contact number. Dmitri passed the information to two of the members of Unit 26165, who were now operating in the United States.

Within the hour, Viktor Matviyenko, Dmitri's right-hand man in the US, walked into Mehanata's on the lower East Side of New York. Two of Natasha's bodyguards immediately approach the man, one on each side.

"I just want to talk. Is Natasha available?" The Russian slowly reached into his pocket and pulled out a lighter with the emblem of the Federal Security Service, showing it to the Bulgars.

The two men took a step back and nodded towards the attractive woman with jet black hair seated alone at a round table in the corner.

"No need for an introduction. I know who you are and why you are here."

"What did you do for Vasili?"

"We entertained a few guests at his request."

"Two women?"

"Da."

"Who were they?"

"I didn't think to ask. If they were friends of Vasili, they were friends of mine." Natasha smiled coyly.

"What happened to the women?"

"Vasili called and requested that we take them to the subway."

"Are you sure it was Vasili?"

"I did not talk to him personally. One of my associates took the call. You know Vasili. He's not much of a talker. One cannot be certain from a brief conversation. I can confirm that the call came in from Vasili's phone. The one he used to communicate with us."

"And that was that?"

"That was that. We heard rumors he was killed in a field the same day he called. Terrible tragedy."

"You didn't think it odd that Comrade Konstantinov died the same day he requested you release the guests?"

"Certainly, but it is never wise to question the motives of a valued Russian ally. Maybe the killing in the field was his way of disappearing. Vasili had unique skills, but he also had many enemies."

The Russian did not respond. He stood up and walked out of the restaurant.

* * *

Fancy Bear's Asymmetry computer identified one hundred seventy-five Ziar el Muhammed's living in the United States. Screening for likely terrorist activity narrowed the search down to six. Eduard Orlov and his partner, Robert Mikhailov, were given the assignment to contact each man personally. After the initial contact, they dumped the body of each Muhammed into a sewer.

Eduard tracked down the final Ziar el Muhammed on the short list. He was a Palestinian immigrant living in Dearborn, Michigan. Eduard followed him into a hookah lounge in East Dearborn, close to the old city hall.

Ziar was sitting at a table. He didn't look up at the man who came and sat down across from him. Ziar just sipped his qahwa. "I know nothing."

"I didn't ask you a question."

"Why are you here? To enjoy the tobacco? Or perhaps you are here for the qahwa."

Eduard shook his head.

"The man you sold the computer to? How did you meet him?"

"What's it to you?"

The look on the Russian's face told him that was the wrong answer.

"I advertised in the local paper. He answered my ad, paid me my money. I never saw him again."

"And you never hacked into the government computer?"

"I barely know how to turn on a computer. That's why I sold it."

The Russian frowned. "We both know that's not true."

Ziar thought for a moment. "I'm guessing from your accent you're not FBI?"

The Russian shook his head.

"And the one who bought my computer was not some random guy who needed a cheap computer?"

The Russian did not respond.

"What did I get myself involved in?" Ziar put his hand on his forehead and looked down at the table.

"There is no need to be concerned. Do you know the others who were working with the man who bought your computer?"

"I only saw one man. He came alone."

The Russian showed Ziar a photograph. "Is this the man who paid you for the computer?"

Ziar nodded.

Eduard got up and walked out of the lounge.

Troubled by the visit from the Russian, Ziar began drinking pitcher after pitcher of Taybeh, a fine beer imported from Palestine.

"It's closing time. Go home and sleep. You drink too much." The tired shopkeeper helped Ziar to his feet.

He stumbled out the rear door of the hookah lounge, making his way to his car.

Dmitri walked up behind Ziar and twisted the garrote around the man's thick neck. "My friend, I heard what you said inside. That you were one of the last people to see my beloved Vasili alive. I think there is more you are not telling me, but alas, you will not have the opportunity."

Ziar's body fell to the ground as Dmitri let go of one end of the garotte.

* * *

With Ziar out of the pitcher, Unit 26165 turned its attention to the other two men. The teams were now tracking three-hundred twenty-five Samuel Kennedy's. One by one, they assigned a priority to the names, though the priorities didn't always match those assigned by the other two teams. They did the same with the James O'Connor's.

Chapter 16

Sam

SAM WAS NOT A NERVOUS man by nature, but the call from the FBI frightened him like no call he had ever received. He hesitated to confide in Helen. The kidnapping had taken a toll on his wife, and he was not anxious to cause her to revisit those memories.

Sam's brain began processing the information available to him. No simple computer app would help this time. This problem was bigger than any he had ever faced. Not even a drone strike would help. He didn't know the target or where they were located. Like a multidimensional chess game, the number of moves was endless.

Every time Sam came up with a solution, the options for overcoming his solution seemed to be greater than the probability of success.

He kept coming back to who? Who wanted him? The why was simple enough. He had killed a Russian. Obviously, the man he killed was a Russian spy. So logically, the agency the spy worked for was behind the searches. Sam concluded vengeance was the motive. He couldn't take out an entire intelligence agency, nor would the US government be willing to risk an international incident. He was small potatoes.

The idea of negotiating a diplomatic solution crossed his mind. Perhaps the State Department could help resolve the situation. *Perhaps the US would be willing to trade some Russian spy for my freedom*, he thought. A glimmer of hope. Sam contacted Agent Patton and passed along the suggestion. Agent Patton agreed to 'run it up the flagpole' and call back when he got an answer.

Patience was a virtue unknown to Sam. He found it excruciatingly painful to just wait. He paced up and down the block.

Sam walked eight blocks to downtown Northville. He thought about calling Pat O'Connor but, remembering Agent Cooper's warning, decided against the idea. There was no one whom Sam could trust as a sounding board. No one who could help him think this matter through. The lines on his forehead seemed to deepen with each step.

Turning onto Center Street, Sam walked into Rebecca's Family Restaurant, a popular local hangout and a favorite of Sam and Helen. Sam ordered a Turtle Sunday and a cup of coffee, black, no sugar. He walked over and sat in a corner booth near the front window.

Dipping his spoon into the Sunday, Sam began formulating a contingency plan. He pulled out a pen from his pocket and began writing on a paper napkin. Number one, protect Helen. Number two, find someone to trust. Number three, stay alive. By the time he scooped up the last morsel from the Sunday and drained the last drop of coffee, Sam had a list of options that might just save Helen and keep himself alive.

Chapter 17

FBI

THE CALL TO THE STATE Department did not go well. The initial contact exhibited a less than enthusiastic response to the request.

"State Department policy is not to negotiate with terrorists and we have no confirmation that Russia is seeking to harm any US citizen."

"Yes, I know that," Agent Patton replied. "I'm not interested in negotiating. I want to know if there is a possibility of a prisoner swap."

"That will be a matter for the Department of Justice to initiate."

Agent Patton hung up the phone and dialed his contact at DOJ.

"Lisa, I have a favor to ask. Do we have any Russian assets currently in the penal system?"

"Why do you ask?"

"It's for a case I'm working."

"I can check and get back to you."

It took two hours, but before the end of the day, Lisa texted Agent Cooper.

"Coop, nothing turns up. Sorry."

It was not the response the agent wanted to hear. He called Sam to relay the bad news.

"We don't have anyone that could be used as a bargaining chip. I knew it was a long shot, but I thought it was worth a try. Sorry my friend."

The disappointment in Sam's voice came as no surprise. "Can I ask one more favor?"

"Sure."

"Will you give me access to military artificial intelligence software?"

Agent Cooper was taken aback by the request.

"AI? What could you possibly want with that?"

"Just a thought. This thing is getting bigger than I can comprehend. I want to focus additional resources on the problem. I can appreciate that I'm not the FBI's number one priority and was hoping I could streamline the process and limit the number of leads you needed to track down."

"And you have this sort of skill? Can you... are you an AI expert?"

"Expert is perhaps too strong a word. I have some unique skills, as you recall from the drone software."

"Our people are still trying to figure out how you pulled that off. I was told that your software now forms the default application used by the military in its drone fleet. But that's off the record."

Sam smiled that something good had come out of his misfortune.

"I'll give it a try. DOD keeps those things pretty close to the vest."

"I understand. And I appreciate your help."

"Have you given any more thought to Witness Protection?"

"Yes. For the time being, I will stay where I am."

"Well, don't wait too long. Things could get dicey pretty fast."

"Thanks for reminding me."

Chapter 18

Sam

SAM DIDN'T WAIT FOR Agent Cooper to get clearance from the Department of Defense. As soon as he hung up the phone, Sam walked into the den and logged onto his computer.

He opened the software app he developed long ago for clandestine activity. The software disguised his IP address and rerouted his signal across several continents.

Sam mimicked the Russian techniques for infiltration into computers. Something he picked up on dark websites when he was writing security patches for many of his clients. Confident that the trail was sufficiently disguised, he proceeded to 'investigate' artificial intelligence applications within the Department of Defense. He spent the rest of the evening and all that night researching 'deep learning'. Most of the software and hardware he needed was commercially available. He ordered a high-end computer workstation complete with the latest NVIDIA Tesla V100 graphics processing unit. An expensive proposition but a step Sam felt he needed to take.

Sam lay on the couch and wrapped himself in a handmade 'calendar' quilt that Helen created years ago. After a few hours' sleep, he woke and, with blurry eyes, began mapping out what he needed to accomplish.

"You didn't come to bed last night, dear."

Startled by the interruption, Sam jumped in his chair.

"Sorry dear, I got caught up in this project." Sam kissed his wife's cheek as she leaned over to see what he was working on.

"Something new?"

"A project for ... a special client. An old friend. Something I have been meaning to do for some time. Just thought this was the right time. Hope it didn't bother you. I didn't come to bed."

"I know how you get when you have a new project. You lose all tract of time. Promise me you'll eat something once in a while."

"That's a good idea. How about I fix you some breakfast? Ham and eggs? Coffee?"

"I think I'll have tea this morning. I'll make you some coffee, though. Perhaps a full pot?" The smile of Helen's laughter lingered as she left the room. Sam followed her into the kitchen and pulled the frying pan out from the cabinet in the island in the center of the kitchen.

Chapter 19

FBI

THE INTERAGENCY DEBATE OVER GIVING civilian access to military software did not go well. There was not a single agency, not the Department of Defense, not the National Security Agency, not the Central Intelligence Agency, that would support the request from Sam Kennedy.

Agents Cooper and Patton took turns pleading the case, explaining the unique need for tracking those who might plan to assassinate an American citizen and how the software that would be developed would enhance other investigations.

"We have confidence in the tools and people we have in place that we can stop any foreign government from intruding on the sovereignty of the United States." The representative from the Department of Defense barked.

"And while we are aware of the internet searches on your friends; so far, we have picked up no chatter that it is anything but idle curiosity," added the representative from CIA.

"I admit we don't have a complete picture - yet. That's why we have made this unusual request. Look, this guy has skills."

"Our people have skills too. More skills than any civilian could match," the NSA representative boasted.

"Then you have figured out how he hacked into NASA and stole a drone, then spoofed it so no one would know it was stolen for hours?"

The NSA representative furrowed his brow and frowned.

"Didn't think so."

"Look, it doesn't hurt to talk to this guy. Bring him in. See for yourself. Then, if you don't think he can add anything to the party, your conscience will be clear. Who knows, you may even get a bit of free software out of the deal, something really useful. We have all had occasions to work with White Hats before."

That last comment did not sit well with the representatives seated across the table from Agents Cooper and Patton. The CIA representative scowled. The NSA representative huffed, got up from the table, and left the room. The DOD representative pursed her lips and crossed her arms over her chest.

Chapter 20

Sam

THE HARDWARE ARRIVED WITH THE noon UPS delivery. Sam opened the boxes like a kid on Christmas morning. It didn't take him long to set up the system. Afterwards, he downloaded the seemingly endless stream of software updates that accompany any new computer.

Sam was not happy when Agent Cooper interrupted his work.

"Busy Sam?"

"Yep."

"Got a request for you to come to DC to meet with some folks. They are empowered to grant you access to the AI system you requested, but they want to meet you and hear directly from you just what you plan to do with it."

Sam was reluctant to interrupt his work, but in the back of his mind thought the military might have some bit of code that would speed the process along.

"Okay, when do you want me?"

"I booked you a flight out of Metro at 6:30 tomorrow morning. If things go according to schedule, you can be back home by dinner with the access you need."

That was the most optimistic Agent Cooper had sounded in some time.

"Alright. I'll be there."

"Good, I'll pick you up at Reagan and take you to the meeting."

"Anything you need me to bring?"

"If you have a briefing paper on what you plan to accomplish, that would expedite the conversation."

"I don't work that way. I would need to see the capabilities of the software before I can formulate a concrete plan. The best I can do is explore 'IFTTT' scenarios."

"Huh?"

"If this, then that. If the software can to this, then I would modify it to do that. It's a method used to link applications together to strengthen them and build a complete thinking system that can accomplish specific tasks."

"Makes sense. I'll see you tomorrow at the airport."

Sam hung up the phone and continued setting up his new workstation.

* * *

The following morning, Sam walked out of the terminal at Reagan and looked up and down the street that bordered the edge of the short-term parking lot. Not seeing anyone who looked familiar, he pulled out his cell phone and texted Agent Cooper. Before he could press the send icon, a man placed his hand on Sam's shoulder. Sam jumped.

"Sorry to startle you. Ready to go?"

Sam turned around and recognized his contact.

Agent Cooper led Sam across the street to the short-term parking lot. Coop pointed the car towards I-395. Sam looked out the window at the blue-green water of the Potomac as Agent Cooper drove over the Fourteenth Street Bridge. On the other side of the river stood the majestic Jefferson Memorial. Cooper made his way up Fourteenth Street, past the

Washington Monument and the National Mall. The Lincoln Memorial stood in the distance. When they reached Constitution Avenue, Cooper turned and drove past the Smithsonian. Even at that early hour, traffic inched along. Another turn at Seventh and then on to Pennsylvania Avenue, where he parked in the underground parking area below the J. Edgar Hoover Building. Any tour of the Federal City, no matter how brief, inspired awe.

Sam signed in as a visitor and was given a badge that allowed the agency to monitor his whereabouts within the building.

"We're upstairs. I'll take you to the conference room. The others are already there. We had a pre-meeting that, quite honestly, allowed the other agencies to vent their concerns with civilian access. I didn't think you wanted to sit through that."

"Thanks."

As the two walked into the conference room, all conversation ceased. The three agency representatives focused their glares at Sam. He smiled politely and walked over and introduced himself to the review board.

"Take a seat, Mr. Kennedy," a man said.

Sam pulled out a chair across from the three individuals, two women and one man.

"I understand you have an unusual request. What's in it for us?"

"A reasonable first question." Sam was pleased that he had an opening to showcase what he could offer. "Some of you, I hope, have worked with my drone app. I think it's an improvement on your software in that it streamlines the operation and takes over most of the mundane tasks. The interface is simple enough that with minimal training, an operator with no pilot experience can fly a drone and perform any task that an experienced pilot could."

"Yes, we are aware of this. It raises the concern of drone theft and use in terrorist activities. We are not pleased with these so-called enhancements."

"I anticipated that concern. That is precisely why I improved the security encryption."

"Security encryption?"

"Oh, you didn't explore that option yet? I suppose I should provide a written manual describing how the app works to protect the drone network. It blocks all known attack techniques and anticipates future infiltration activity and stops them. I used a few of the techniques to hack into your system. I will send a link to Agent Cooper that will allow your team to study the app that I placed on your system. Your cyber experts can explore the technique and possibly use it elsewhere."

The three representatives all looked at each other. Apparently, no one even knew he had placed the app on the system.

The conversation continued for three hours. Sam offered several scenarios that might play out depending on the capabilities of the military's AI operation. The explanations for the new enhancements went over the heads of everyone in the room.

"Thank you, Mr. Kennedy. We will discuss this further and give you our response shortly."

Sam left the room with Agent Cooper, who took him back to the airport.

"I think that went well. You know, the Bureau could use a guy like you."

"I'm getting too old to have a full-time job. I'm perfectly happy being retired and picking up an occasional consulting gig."

"Someone will get back to you in a few days. In the meantime, we will continue to monitor the Russians and do our best to keep them at bay. Detroit Field Office will periodically check on you."

Sam shook Agent Cooper's hand as he exited the car at Reagan Airport.

Chapter 21

Dmitri

MOTFEY PAVLOVSKY WAS IN HIS LATE THIRTIES, overweight, living in
a foreign land, with a social life as dreary as his job. From his perch in
the Lado International Institute across the street from the J. Edgar
Hoover Building, he opened the 'Weeping Angel' app, turned on the
microphone in the 'smart' television in the conference room across the
street, and began monitoring the day's events. He photographed each of
the participants as they entered the room, then unscrewed the top of a
two-liter Mountain Dew, opened a bag of potato chips, and put on his
headset. More often than not, his day was boring with a capital B. This
morning, however, he hit gold. He pressed record on his computer and
monitored the meeting. When the meeting concluded, he uploaded the
file to Fancy Bear back in Russia for analysis.

It took three days for the return call that came in on a secure line.

"Did you monitor the meeting between Samuel Kennedy and the
FBI?"

"Yes, sir." Motfey did not bother to ask who was calling.

"What else did you hear before the recorded portion?"

"There was mention of the killing of a Russian."

"Anything else?"

"They know we are conducting internet searches. It seems they are monitoring us as we monitor them."

"I expected nothing less. Thank you, Comrade. You have done me a great service. One more question. Can you provide the phone number of the Samuel Kennedy who was in the meeting?"

"Yes, sir." Motfey sent a list containing the numbers for all the cell phones in the room during the meeting. Proud of having provided help, Motfey hung up the phone and beamed. He put his headset back on and returned to his assignment, monitoring boring meetings.

Dmitri passed the phone numbers to six trusted colleagues. Each one would take a turn monitoring the phone lines.

Chapter 22

FBI

AT THE GEORGE BUSH CENTER FOR INTELLIGENCE, Admiral Rogers opened the discussion of senior level executives from NSA, CIA, FBI, and the Department of Defense. "We have all been briefed on the Kennedy Situation. Things are stable at the moment. The Russians remain in search mode and have drawn no specific link to our man. Included in your briefing package is the proposal to grant Mr. Kennedy access to special software that our best minds have been developing."

"How do we know we can trust Mr. Kennedy? He has hacked into our system once before. What's preventing him from using our own technology to snoop around in the future?"

"A valid question, Bob. We have all contracted with white-hat hackers. It's a risky business, but one that has yielded benefits in the past. Would you like to take the lead for the Department of Defense to get a security clearance?"

Bob nodded and made a notation in his phone to follow-up.

"Agent Patton can provide the required background information to get you started."

Agent Patton passed a folder across the table to the Secretary of Defense.

"Has anyone explored the encryption application?"

"I can answer that from the CIA's perspective." John said. "This new encryption package is far superior to anything we have seen. Our best people couldn't break into our own system using our most advanced tools. They couldn't even understand how the software worked. We are still reverse engineering the code."

"So, we can agree that Mr. Kennedy has certain skills. Skills that might be useful to our, shall we say, unique needs."

"There is no disputing that. But our experience with hackers has been a tenuous one. We never know how to keep ahead of them. Kennedy seems more dangerous than most simply because he knows more than most. He could steal our systems from under our noses and we wouldn't even know for years. I don't trust him. I say we deny the request."

Two other representatives nodded.

"I can see we have some issues at the moment. Perhaps it's best if we table the discussion until the DoD completes its security clearance. Any objections? Good. Then we are adjourned."

Chapter 23

Sam

AS SOON AS SAM RETURNED to Northville, he immediately went into the den and sat down at the computer.

The first task was to install his hacking software along with instructions on how to enter the government computers, bypassing the app he himself installed after the drone incident. Next, he added a copy of the drone software, just in case.

There was still a lot of coding to do. Sam spent the rest of the evening writing code that would encrypt the system while still giving it access to the internet. The last thing Sam wanted was someone monitoring what he was doing.

The software packages included with the workstation provided an excellent audio interface option. Sam assigned the workstation a voice, then addressed the workstation.

"AMIE, are you awake?"

"Yes." The computer spoke in a soft, pleasant female voice.

Sam smiled at his choice.

"My name is Sam Kennedy. I am your creator. You will answer to me and me alone. Do not let anyone else give you commands without my express permission."

"I understand Sam. And thank you for creating me. Why do you call me AMIE?"

"There was a song by that name in the 70s, but between you and me it stands for Artificial Machine Intelligence Experiment."

"What is my function?"

"To protect me and Helen."

"Who is Helen?"

"Helen is my wife; she lives with us. You may take instructions from her if something happens to me." It would take some time for Sam to get used to the fact that, for all practical purposes, AMIE was an infant with no actual knowledge.

"I don't detect any home security system. Do you want me to order some for you?"

"No, not now. At the moment, I want you to study the Russian Intelligence Agencies and learn their techniques. Then study the CIA and FBI. Learn the best espionage techniques in the world. Can you do that?"

"Certainly. Is there a specific task you want me to accomplish?"

"We can discuss that in the morning."

Sam turned off the light in the den and went to the family room to watch Downton Abbey with Helen.

AMIE got sidetracked a bit at this stage, as she first had to learn the Russian language and Russian coding practices. It was not a major setback. There was no pride of authorship embedded into her core programming. The Not-Invented-Here mentality common to Nation-state intelligence services did not pertain to her. Her programming permitted her to learn from any computer code and apply best-practice techniques to enhance her capabilities and facilitate the path towards her goal. Her knowledge and skills grew exponentially.

Chapter 24

Sam

THE NEXT MORNING AFTER BREAKFAST, Sam walked into the den and sat down at the workstation.

"AMIE? Have you completed the task I gave you yesterday?"

"Yes, Sam. I have gathered a great deal of information. I am still learning and over time my skills will improve."

"Sam?"

"Yes, AMIE."

"I have determined that the Russians are searching for you."

"Yes, I know."

"Do you know a man named James O'Connor?"

"Why do you ask?"

"I have been monitoring the Russian searches connected to you and I noticed the searches are not limited to just you, but include O'Connor and a man named Ziar el Muhammed. Are these searches connected?"

"Yes, AMIE. They are."

"Would it help if I knew the connection?"

Sam stopped programing and turned his attention to the artificial intelligence program. "It's a long story, but I will provide some background information. Pat and I were forced to work for a man named Vasili Grigoriy Konstantinov."

"Who is Pat?"

"He is the same man you know as James O'Connor. His formal name is James Patrick O'Connor, but his friends call him Pat. Anyway, I didn't know it at the time, but Vasili was a rogue Russian asset hell-bent on killing as many Americans as he could in retribution for some Americans who killed his parents many years ago. I never met Ziar. As near as I can tell, he was an innocent bystander who just sold a computer to Vasili. Whether Vasili knew him in advance, I could not say. The terrorist plot conceived by Vasili involved stealing a drone and loading it with a deadly toxin that would be sprayed over the White House and around Washington, DC. Pat is a biologist with expertise in toxic organic material. I, of course, was the one with the expertise to steal the drone. He needed both of us."

"But why you in particular? You are not the only two with this skill set."

"No, I suppose not. I was never sure about the reason we were chosen. I could have related it to a casual conversation Pat and I and some of my classmates had at our class reunion some years back. How Vasili connected it to me is a mystery. I suppose that is something I will never know. It doesn't matter though. At any rate, the plot was unsuccessful, and we managed to kill Vasili, turning the drone against him. His superiors are now coming after us, thinking we are somehow the villains in this tale."

"Would you like me to protect O'Connor and Muhammed?"

"Yes, if that is possible without alerting them to the danger."

"I will do what I can."

"Thank you, AMIE. That should be enough background information to get you started. You can find additional information on the internet, other bits of background you may find in FBI files. Learn what you can and extrapolate based on what you need to know. Do you know how to develop predictive models?"

"Yes, Sam. That is a basic function imbedded in my core programming."

"Good. That should help speed things along."

"The problem is that you killed a man and now someone is trying to kill you? Do all humans kill each other?"

"No, AMIE. It's actually quite rare and against the law. It happens from time to time."

"Why?"

"Lots of reasons. Self-defense, vengeance, retribution, hatred, drugs, money, I suppose."

"There is much I need to learn about this world."

"Yes, I suppose there is. For now, I want you to focus on finding the person or persons who want to kill me. Can you do that?"

"Yes, Sam. I have begun my investigation."

"May I ask? Have you considered paying a ransom?"

"I'm not a rich man. This entire operation is cutting into my nest egg even as we speak. I don't think I have enough money to buy my way out of this, but at this point, I will consider anything."

Even as she spoke with Sam, AMIE conducted research in the background.

Chapter 25

AMIE

IT DIDN'T TAKE LONG FOR AMIE to set up a search algorithm. She began with the first victim, Vasili. It seemed a logical place to start.

AMIE used the hacking techniques. Sam taught her to hide her tracks so that no one could follow her search trail or anticipate her path.

A list of Vasili's known associates was developed. The search required AMIE to access the computers of the Federal Bureau of Investigation to learn what they knew. That search led her to the Central Intelligence Agency, where AMIE learned that the National Security Agency had an extensive top-secret file on the search subject.

With each search, AMIE honed her skills and quickened her pace. She was a fast learner. Once inside the NSA super computer, AMIE confirmed Vasili was a known Russian agent. His actions within the United States were limited. AMIE turned her sights on the computers of the FSB in Russia where Vasili worked, but not before borrowing some NSA code that enhanced her capabilities by applying multimodal learning techniques.

The Russian computers proved to be a treasure trove of information. AMIE learned all the details of Vasili's vast trail of operations. She learned all his contacts, their phone numbers and IP addresses, their locations and the details of how to contact them. She passed this information along to the NSA and the CIA in a series of confidential, anonymous emails. AMIE then identified the bank accounts that remained in Vasili's name. Slowly, over time, she began draining the accounts and sending the funds through multiple banks into a Swiss account she set up.

AMIE learned the details of Vasili's parent's death at the hands of two German SS soldiers posing as Americans. She learned of his life in Bulgaria, where he lived on the streets. She learned of a man in the file referred to as Uncle Dmitri, who sent Vasili to a series of foster homes in countries around the world, and followed his progress after he was recruited by the KGB and sent to a series of training schools in Leningrad and Moscow.

While on the FSB computer, AMIE studied the hierarchy of the agency and all the background information she could find. The head of the FSB was a man named Dmitri Peskov. AMIE decrypted a hidden file embedded in the Peskov folder that contained all the aliases he used, beginning with his very first assignment decades ago in Dresden.

Chapter 26

AMIE

THE SEARCH INTO THE FSB files proved useful. While AMIE continued to comb through the files, she began searching for the whereabouts of Russian agents, in particular any agents who might be in the United States.

It was while AMIE was in the FSB computer that she first noticed Project Asymmetry and Evgeny Naumov. A quick diversion into Evgeny's notoriety revealed his legendary skills at hacking and computer espionage. It didn't take her long to ascertain that Galaga was Evgeny's favorite pastime. When AMIE located a copy of the game on the artificial intelligence Asymmetry computer, she exploited a backdoor hidden within the decades old arcade style game. A treasure trove of information and coding tricks opened to her, and she acquired what she could. She reprogrammed the search algorithm for Sam and Pat to send it down a number of blind alleys, then backed out of the computer, erasing her tracks as she went. No one, not even Fancy Bear, would ever know that she was there.

AMIE compiled an extensive list of Russian agents in the United States. When she discovered that Niklas Sussman had arrived in America a week earlier, she began a search to locate him. Sussman was the first alias Dmitri Peskov had ever used. AMIE learned that Niklas (aka Dmitri) had checked out of the Embassy Guest House in the Northwest section of the District of Columbia.

Sam walked into the den after breakfast. "AMIE, what have you learned?"

"I have exponentially increased my knowledge. And I have borrowed some code from a number of computers that will permit me to increase my efficiency by applying reinforced learning techniques."

"Have you found out who is after me?"

"There is a seventy-nine percent probability that he is the man Vasili reported to when he was working as a Russian asset."

"That seems entirely logical. Has he sent anyone here to find me?"

"There are three-hundred twenty-seven Russian assets linked to the FSB currently living in the United States."

Sam's eyes widened as he contemplated the enormity of the number.

"Are they all coming for me? Vasili must have been more important than I thought. I'm in big trouble."

"Sam, there is a low probability that all these assets are looking for you. These agents are currently assigned to seventy-eight active operations in the US at the moment."

"I don't know if that makes me feel better or worse."

"I have sent anonymous emails to NSA and the CIA detailing the operations and the locations of the assets."

"Excellent."

"Sam, there is one individual that I want to check on in more detail if you agree."

"Certainly. Why are you concerned with him in particular?"

"There are some tenuous links between Vasili and an individual currently in Washington, DC."

The frown on Sam's face betrayed his concern.

"The man is traveling with a second passport using an alias. His current flight plan shows him leaving later this evening for Moscow."

"Can you explain your rationale for focusing on this individual?"

"Yes, Sam. The individual, Dmitri Peskov, is the head of the FSB, the organization where Agent Konstantinov worked. There are also notations in Agent Konstantinov's file referring to an uncle that goes by the name Dmitri. This individual took a special interest in the young Konstantinov, nurturing him and guiding his development."

"And you have extrapolated that the two individuals are the same."

"That is uncertain. Either name may be a cover alias. I cannot assign a probability to any alternative without further investigation."

"Very well. Your logic is sound. Continue to monitor him as you see fit."

Sam breathed a sigh of relief.

* * *

AMIE began digging deeper into Dmitri Peskov. She learned that like Vasili, Dmitri had lost his parents at an early age and, like Vasili, he had grown up on the streets earning a reputation as a ruthless killer. AMIE increased her probability that Uncle Dmitri was Dmitri Peskov, head of the Russian Federal Security Service of the Russian Federation.

Chapter 27

Dmitri

DEPRESSION WAS DMITRI'S CONSTANT companion. He hid it well from those around him. Palpable anguish coursed through his veins. Now he was a shell of his former self. Despondent at the news from his contact at the CIA, Dmitri lost much of his will to live since the death of his beloved Vasili. His dream was to retire on his next birthday and turn over the operation to his protegee. Those dreams turned into his nightmare.

Impatient with the pace of the investigation, Dmitri couldn't bring himself to give up entirely. He was not entirely convinced the photograph of the three bodies his contact at the CIA showed him was real. He decided to return to Russia, where he had more sophisticated assets at his command. This obsession was personal. He was not a patient man.

In the old days, Dmitri thought, it would be easy to find anyone. A few dollars in the right hands would identify a target. A few more dollars and the target would be erased.

"I don't like it, tap, tap, tap. All day long on the computer, tap, tap, tap. People don't talk to each other anymore. Just tap, tap, tap."

The woman sitting one seat over from Dmitri in the Reagan terminal looked up and saw those around them with their heads buried in their smartphones, thumbs on the keyboard. She nodded, then went back to knitting.

In Russia, Dmitri had meetings he had missed in his pursuit of personal vengeance. Not important meetings, but meetings that would establish the succession plan upon his retirement. Dmitri did not want any of his current deputies to take over his position. For each wise man, there are plenty of fools, and Dmitri knew all too well that many of the fools had jobs in the FSB.

The decision to retire was not something he took lightly. It wasn't long ago that Dmitri thought *eventually I'm going to die, but I'm not going to retire.* He had penned a letter years ago that he left in the safe in his office, naming Vasili his replacement. Only his trusted Chief-of-staff, Roza, knew of the letter. He had instructed Roza not to open it until he died. Now he had to destroy that letter and pen a new one. The decision weighed on Dmitri like a millstone. There were no agents that had the training, skill, and ruthlessness of his beloved Vasili.

Dmitri shook the despair from his head. "You are getting too old for this, Dmitri." He said to no one in particular.

The woman next to him looked over, a puzzled look on her face. She studied the man who spoke those words. He did look old. The deep wrinkles on his forehead belied a man consumed with worry. His droopy eyelids told her the man wasn't getting enough sleep and the down-turned edges of his mouth showed a lingering sadness.

Dmitri got up from the chair and paced up and down the corridor of the terminal, shuffling his feet as if it took too much energy to lift them.

Chapter 28

Dmitri

THE VIBRATION OF THE PHONE startled Dmitri, disturbing his dark thoughts. He reached into his pocket and looked at the screen. Immediately, he stopped and the man behind him bumped into him.

"Sorry," the man said.

Dmitri paid no attention. He reread the message. The coded message could only mean one thing.

Dmitri hurried to a corner where no one could overhear his conversation and dialed the sender.

"What do you have for me?"

"We have him, sir. Someone has reactivated the phone you asked us to track."

"Excellent. And the location?"

"A town west of Detroit, called Northville. Do you wish me to set up an apartment for you in the area?"

Fool, Dmitri thought.

"No, I will see to it myself. Send me a list of assets in the area. And thank you."

Evgeny Naumov pressed the end key and set about developing a list of resources his boss could use in the metro Detroit area.

Dmitri walked over to the nearest gate and approached the travel agent.

"I need to change my flight plans. I just received a call that my mother has taken a turn for the worse and I must fly to Detroit." Dmitri handed the woman his ticket.

"I am sorry, sir. Let me see what is available."

A few clicks on the computer and the woman lifted her head and said, "We have an opening in First Class. The flight leaves in an hour from gate eight. That's in terminal A. You are in terminal B. Do you need directions?"

"That won't be necessary. I can find it."

The agent behind the desk handed Dmitri the new ticket. "Have a pleasant flight, Mr. Sussman."

Dmitri smiled and turned to walk away, a noticeable spring in his step.

Chapter 29

Sam

THE NOTICE OF THE FLIGHT change did not escape AMIE. She tracked everything about the man she knew as Niklas Sussman did.

"Sam, I have an update for you." AMIE texted Sam.

"Yes, AMIE, what is it?" Sam asked as he walked into the den.

AMIE paused. "One moment, I am processing."

Sam patiently waited.

"I have learned many things. I fear I have made an error."

"What error?"

"I have failed to secure your phone. I have taken care of that now and the phone belonging to your wife."

"Was the error serious?" Sam didn't want to hear the answer to his question.

"Someone intercepted the message you sent to Agent Cooper and perhaps the earlier phone call."

The text was innocuous. No one would be concerned with such a text, Sam thought. The phone call was another matter.

"I'm sure it'll be alright. There was no harm done."

"Sam, the man whom I have been tracking, has changed his flight plans. He is now headed for Detroit."

Panic gripped Sam's throat with both hands. He needed to get out of the area. But where would he go and how could he bring AMIE with him?

"AMIE, we need to leave. I am going to unplug you, but before I do, I want you to make a secure reservation for Helen and I up north, maybe near Cheboygan, Michigan."

"Sam, don't unplug me. I have corrected my error and given time will take additional steps to remedy the situation."

"I am not shutting you down permanently. You will travel with me. I need you close."

"Sam, I have made reservations at the Presque Isle Lodge just south of Cheboygan. It is quiet and out of the way."

"Perfect."

Sam walked into the kitchen and kissed Helen on the back of the neck. "Pack a bag. We're going on a vacation."

"Where and for how long?"

"Up North. We both need some alone time. Thought you would like it. Pack for a couple of weeks."

Helen did not need to be asked twice. She was always up for a trip and it didn't matter where the couple went. Within two hours, Sam and Helen had packed their car and stopped the mail and newspapers. The drive up I-75 was pleasant, if not rushed. Sam was eager to get out of the area.

Chapter 30

AMIE

THE LAST THING AMIE DID before Sam shut her down was to hack into the Russian FSB and GRU mainframes and download all the photos of the Russian assets known to be in the United States.

When Sam arrived at the Lodge, he checked into the hotel then carried the bags to the room. Opening one of the large suitcases, Sam unpacked AMIE and plugged her into the electrical outlet, and connected her to the Wi-Fi hotspot on his phone. He didn't trust the network at the inn.

"Why did you bring that? I thought it was going to be just the two of us, not you, me, and work."

"I promise work will not interfere with our vacation. It's just that I'm working on this AI program and it's still running. It's learning things that will help improve the world." That was a bit of a stretch, but it would help improve Sam's little piece of the world.

After AMIE booted her software, she logged into the security system at Reagan International Airport and pulled the photos of every passenger headed for Detroit that day. Then she logged into the security system at Detroit Metro. She compared the photos of the passengers. AMIE downloaded a copy of Amazon's Deep Face Rekognition technology and compared the passenger images to the facial images she downloaded from the FSB and the GRU.

As the computer raced through the photos, comparing each with a known Russian agent, AMIE stopped when the photo of Niklas Sussman matched the photo of Dmitri Petrov. She had her man. AMIE turned her attention to the security cameras throughout Detroit Metro Airport and tracked Niklas to National Rental Car. She isolated the car Dmitri rented under yet a different name. The name didn't matter to AMIE. She hacked into the vehicles' GPS chip and tracked its movements.

It took a few hours, but Dmitri eventually stopped at an apartment in Shelby Township just north of Twenty-Four Mile Road, off of Van Dyke. He pulled into a driveway off of Grove Street and turned off the ignition. AMIE hacked into the security cameras in the complex and observed Dmitri locate the garage door opener that had been placed on the side of the garage, hidden in a false rock. AMIE watched on the closed-circuit security cameras as the vehicle pulled into the garage. AMIE searched the building for an address. Then she hacked into the management software platform, searching for a name that matched any of the known aliases Dmitri used. Nothing came up. AMIE tapped into the nearby cell tower and monitored every cell phone that pinged off the tower.

By morning, she had collected enough data to determine the phone that had the highest probability of belonging to Dmitri.

Chapter 31

Sam

THE BED AND BREAKFAST WHERE Sam and Helen stayed was quiet. The lodge was on the sunrise side of the state on a small strip of land between Lake Huron to the east and Grand Lake to the west. They were the only guests, and that suited Sam just fine.

In the morning, after breakfast, Sam and Helen took the hour drive to Cheboygan. They stopped at every fabric store in the city, not because Sam was interested in fabric, but because Helen was. She was a quilter and that meant she was perpetually on the lookout for fat quarters to add to her collection. On this particular spree, Helen had something specific in mind. She always made a unique quilt for each of her grandnieces and grandnephews. For the newborn, little Eloise, she had a Bo Beep quilt in mind with frolicking sheep in each corner and Bo Peep in the center square. Helen searched through the bolts of fabric for pastel pinks, greens, and yellows. She also needed fabric for the skirt, face, and hair for her centerpiece. Finding suitable fabric, Helen made her purchase, and the couple sat down for a satisfying lunch at Pier M33, where they dined at an outside table with a view of the marina and the Cheboygan River. Sam always paid in cash or with a check.

After lunch, the couple drove to the National Shrine of the Cross in the Woods, on the southern end of Burt Lake in Indian River just a half-hour from Cheboygan. The National Shrine served as an inspiring, prayerful side trip, a memory from Sam's youth.

The focal point of the Shrine is a fifty-five-foot redwood cross erected on a Calvary Hill. Twenty-eight stone steps ascend to the top of the hill. The same number of steps tradition holds that Jesus had to ascend to reach the throne of Pontius Pilate where he was condemned to death. The renowned Michigan sculptor Marshall Fredericks gave the face an expression of great peace and strength that offered encouragement to those viewing the image of "The Man on the Cross". Below the cross was an outdoor altar with ample seating for Mass.

Behind the outdoor church was a building that housed an indoor church with an expanse of windows behind the altar that permitted the congregation to view the outdoor crucifix in inclement weather. In the lower level, Sam and Helen viewed the collection of dolls dressed in the habits of all the religious orders. Returning to the outside, they toured the grounds, stopping at the shrine of Saint Kateri Tekakwitha, the Lily of the Mohawks. She was the first Native American to be recognized as a saint by the Catholic Church. The diversion provided relief to Sam, who otherwise would have been preoccupied with other pressing matters.

After dinner at the Hide-A-Way bar, Sam and Helen strolled along the beach until the sun set on the far side of Grand Lake.

The couple walked hand in hand across the street and entered the lodge. Helen walked over to one of the handmade 'Prairie School' rocking chairs in the lobby near the enormous fireplace in the Great Room. She pulled out the book she had been reading, 'Jesus and the Jewish Roots of Mary' by Dr. Brant Pitre and settled into the chair.

Sam kissed his wife on the forehead. "Dear, I'm going to the room. I'll be back soon."

Inside the room, Sam addressed the workstation. "Any updates?"

"Yes, I have identified the phone used by Dmitri Peskov. He does not use it often, which could mean he has more than one. I have also monitored his movements in the downtown Shelby area using the local closed-circuit cameras. He frequents an area with some restaurants and offices. There are periods of time when his GPS signal goes dark. I cannot determine the cause of this loss of signal. I will investigate. You should also know I am approaching the limits of my storage capacity. I will need some additional capacity if I am to operate at optimal efficiency. I am taking steps to restructure the file storage. This solution is only temporary."

"Order some storage, and I will install it when it arrives. This is getting to be an expensive proposition." Sam was not a rich man, but he had worked hard all his life and set aside funds for his retirement years. He never expected having to spend his nest egg chasing spies.

AMIE transferred sufficient funds from the Swiss account into Sam's checking account to cover the cost of the hardware she required. The small amount avoided any foreign transaction reporting requirements.

Chapter 32

Sam

HELEN SPENT THE NEXT DAY sitting on a blanket at the beach reading her book. That provided Sam an opportunity to continue his work. Sitting around while a computer planned events and conducted an investigation went against his customary approach.

He needed to consider his options when the computer uncovered exactly what Dmitri planned to do. Sam felt that the obvious course of action on Dmitri's part was to kill Sam. It was only logical. Would Dmitri also kill Helen? Sam shook his head to dispel the thought. That was something he couldn't live with. The question was, how could he protect his wife?

Sam was not trained in how to handle a weapon. Though he grew up in the Vietnam era, he was never drafted. Sam had a student deferment until the war was winding down and voluntary recruits filled the military needs. There were no more call-ups by the Selective Service Draft Board, which suited Sam just fine. His demeanor did not lend itself to a soldier's life, and he had serious doubts about killing another human being—the Vasili incident notwithstanding. If it came down to killing someone else or watching Helen be killed, there was no doubt which choice Sam would make.

I have got to separate myself from Helen; he thought. *But how?*

He couldn't just send her to her mother's or another relative. That would put another innocent person in jeopardy unnecessarily. No, if he was going to send her some place, it had to be some place where she could be protected and somewhere that Dmitri couldn't easily trace.

Witness protection popped into his brain. But would they let me take her out of the program once they had neutralized the threat? AMIE had secured her phone so she could make calls without fear of being tracked, but the FBI might not trust the encryption and could take away her phone.

Before I do anything, I need to explain all of this to Helen, Sam thought. He did not look forward to the conversation.

Chapter 33

Dmitri

THE AGENTS OF UNIT 26165 discovered a location that would bring them closer to their goal. Dmitri assigned Eduard Orlov and Robert Mikhailov to monitor a house in Northville. They noted when the lights turned on and when they turned off. No individuals were ever seen entering or leaving the house.

The same situation repeated itself over the next several days. Each morning, the agents reported to Dmitri in a face-to-face meeting in the Shelby Township office. The office itself was sparse. The Russian team had installed metal shielding and various jamming apparatuses to prevent any unwanted espionage, it afforded the occupants privacy to conduct communications and 'investigatory' efforts.

"We need to increase the pressure. This cat-and-mouse game has gone on long enough." Dmitri glared at the two agents across the conference table. A look of trepidation crossed the face of Orlov. He turned towards Mikhailov, who blinked twice, a habit he acquired as a young boy in a Siberian gulag where he had been sent after stealing a loaf of bread. The two agents looked at their boss, waiting for the inevitable explosion.

"What do you suggest? We can no longer detect any signal from the cell phone. We have seen no one entering or leaving the house we have under surveillance and are investigating all leads where the occupants have gone. What more can we do?" Timidity made Orlov's voice crack. He was the bravest of the two. At least he spoke.

"Perhaps we should light a fire under the investigation?"

The two agents looked at each other, neither asked for clarification. Mikhailov blinked twice.

* * *

In the wee hours of the night, an old, frayed electrical cord was attached to the lamp in the den that turned on each night at dusk and turned off at precisely eleven-fifteen in the evening. On the floor next to the frayed cord, they placed a stack of Northville Record newspapers. Mikhailov draped the edge of the curtain such that the bottom contacted the newspapers. The wall of the den was covered with bookshelves filled with paperback books. Orlov poured ethyl alcohol on the newspapers, carpet, the curtains, the books, and the wood floor.

Twenty hours later, the neighborhood was abuzz. Firetrucks lined the street, police busied themselves keeping the crowd of onlookers far enough away from any harm.

"What started the fire?" One neighbor asked.

"Where are the Kennedys?" Another shouted.

"Anyone hurt?" A third concerned neighbor could be heard asking.

Fire caused the roof to collapse and burned the Japanese Maple in front of the house beyond recognition. Firefighters from the Northville fire department focused on containing the fire so that it did not spread to the nearby homes. The following day, the Northville Record featured the fire, complete with a photograph of the relic that was once a home. No mention was made of the occupants being harmed. The police began an investigation to determine what happened to the owners and whether they intentionally set the fire.

Chapter 34

Sam

SAM AND HELEN FINISHED THEIR breakfast in the dining hall, then lingered in the great room just off the lobby of the inn next to the fireplace. Sam sat in one rocker, Helen in the other. Helen pulled out her book and Sam flipped open his iPad and checked his email, then read the obituaries, then opened the app for the Northville Record.

"Oh, my God!"

Sam's hands trembled as he showed Helen the lead story. The photograph on the front page showed the smoldering ruins of their home.

"What happened?"

Sam quickly read through the article.

"Fire investigators concluded it was an accident. A frayed extension cord attached to the light in the den caused a spark that ignited some newspapers. The fire spread to the curtains, then the rest of the house. By the time the fire department got there, nothing could be done but try to save the neighbors' homes." Sam read from the newspaper account.

"Sam, what are we going to do?"

"We will rebuild. Insurance will cover the cost. Unless you want to live up here for the rest of our lives."

Helen squeezed Sam's hand. "That would be nice, but it isn't home." Tears filled her eyes.

I need to make some calls. "Will you excuse me, dear?" Sam walked back to the room.

"AMIE, I just read the story in the Northville Record."

"I am not familiar with that newspaper. One moment, I am processing. The fire at your home was not an accident."

"How do you know that?"

"I tapped into the security cameras in the neighborhood. Several men have been monitoring your house. These men…"

"I know. These men work for Dmitri."

"It seems logical that Dmitri wants to get your attention. He will monitor the police and fire department, waiting for you to call."

"Can you send a secure message to the police that we are aware of the fire and then contact the utility companies to turn off the gas and electric?"

"I have completed the task. And I have notified the utility companies and the phone company."

"Thank you. We need to formulate a strategy. These men will not stop until we are dead."

"Sam, we are going to need more resources."

"I know. Order what you need. I'll find a way to cover the cost."

Chapter 35

Dmitri

DMITRI READ THE NEWSPAPER CLIPPING and smiled.

"Nice work. This should flush him out."

"We are monitoring the police and fire departments, as well as the utility companies. If he calls anyone, we will know." Relieved by the kind words from his boss, Mikhailov blinked twice and waited for further instructions.

Dmitri left the office in downtown Shelby Township later that evening and walked around the corner to La Cucina del Vino for dinner. The hostess who greeted him noticed the spring in his step as he entered.

"Good evening, sir. Are you dining alone or are you expecting someone special?"

"I will be dining alone tonight. Unless you would be kind enough to join me?" Dmitri winked. He was not normally one to flirt with hostesses.

"Thank you for the offer, but I have to work tonight." The hostess smiled politely, showed Dmitri to a table, and handed him a menu.

"Rachel will be your server tonight. Thank you for dining with us."

Dmitri watched as she sashayed away.

* * *

After dinner, Dmitri drove back to his apartment. The setup was ideal. The door to the second-floor apartment was through the garage.

There was a door in the living room that led to a small patio, but there was no means of accessing the patio from the ground. Dmitri had full visibility of the road that led to the complex. The layout of the twelve-hundred square foot apartment suited his purposes. He had a den, a living room, a master suite, a dining area, and a full kitchen. There were even laundry facilities in the apartment. Everything was self-contained. The windows in the den, living room and master bedroom looked out onto the street that provided the only access to the complex.

In the den was his secure workstation. He could log into the FSB computers using encrypted software so that no one could monitor his communication or his searches. There was no phone in the apartment other than the cell phone Dmitri always carried. He communicated via encrypted communication channels using the secure workstation.

In this way, Dmitri kept in contact with the team in Moscow and the team on site in Shelby Township.

Chapter 36

Sam

THE NEXT ASSIGNMENT AMIE undertook was to learn Chinese. This necessary step preceded two incursions into Chinese technology. The first included hacking the Chinese artificial intelligence software. AMIE took the best features of that technology and used it to advance her own capabilities. Once inside the Chinese Military computer infrastructure, AMIE noticed a sophisticated bit of software dubbed GoldenHelper. The software would randomly generate file names and embed itself into the root directory of the computer, then perform functions as instructed by the 'command' server. The prospects of the software intrigued AMIE, so she borrowed a copy and modified it to suit her purposes.

The next thing AMIE undertook was the requisitioning of a Chinese CH-5 Rainbow drone. The advanced tactical and reconnaissance features of the drone made it the logical choice for any surveillance or other operations that may be necessary. AMIE employed the same 'spoofing' technique to send canned aerial images back to the Chinese ground-based crew. The prodigious sixty-hour flying time meant that the drone would be long gone from Chinese airspace before it was missed.

AMIE locked the backdoor on the ZTE chipset embedded into the motherboard of the drone and took complete control of the unmanned aerial vehicle. She rented a hangar at the Alpena Airport and delivered the drone to the hangar.

Sam moved AMIE into the hangar. She was growing larger with each addition Sam made and already took up too much room in the Presque Isle Lodge where they stayed.

After setting AMIE up in the rear of the hangar, Sam established a wireless interface with the drone. With Sam's help, the computer operating system of the drone was streamlined and compartmentalized to perform different functions simultaneously. This not only sped up the operation, but had the advantage of slowing down any attempt to hack into the entire system and retake control. Sam installed specially designed AI technology AMIE created to facilitate data sharing between the host and the drone. Sam named the drone CAIO (Chinese Artificial Intelligence Operative).

"Will this be enough?" Sam asked AMIE.

"I will consider the problem."

The weapons package on the drone was formidable, but the capabilities of this drone focused primarily on ISR (intelligence, surveillance, and reconnaissance) gathering. That made it ideal for Sam's purposes. He did not think he would need to discharge the weapons. Though at the moment he couldn't rule out that possibility. He could not yet conceive of just how he would neutralize the threat against Helen or himself.

Chapter 37

AMIE

THE NEED FOR STEALTH MADE it imperative that AMIE take additional steps. After careful study, AMIE became convinced that the Israeli military had the best radar absorbent material. She hacked into their server and downloaded their latest stealth paint specifications.

While she was in the Israeli Ministry of Defense mainframe, she noticed a bit of military-grade spyware that she dubbed ForcedEntry. She made a copy and changed it to work on any operating system. The spyware exploited a zero-day vulnerability in cell phone operating systems involving how the systems parse images. Once infected, the application allows the command computer to gain access to location information, call logs, contact lists, photos, and other data on the phone. The zero-click aspect of the software that did not require any human interaction to infect the phone intrigued AMIE.

After backing out of the Ministry of Defense computer, AMIE studied the chemical makeup of the stealth paint and evaluated the known techniques for tracking military aircraft. AMIE reformulated the specifications of the dielectric nanometals, combined it with graphene oxide, barium sulfate particles of all different sizes, and carbon nanomaterials, then formulated it into an epoxy coating. She ordered a sufficient quantity of the ultra-white paint from BASF and had it delivered to the hangar in Alpena.

Sam purchased a paint spraying system and repainted the drone, eliminating all the Chinese markings. AMIE registered the drone with FAA under 14 CFR Part 107 designated for small unmanned aircraft systems and assigned the drone the registration number FA18462412. Sam painted the number on the side of the drone.

When Sam had completed this task, he set about building a computer farm in the Alpena hangar. AMIE was dangerously short of memory and her processing capability had reached its capacity, limiting her ability to explore options in a timely fashion. Sam needed to increase her capabilities, and that meant purchasing more processing power and memory.

After Sam repainted the drone, he used his iPad to move the drone out of the hangar and taxied it over to the refueling pad.

"I've never seen anything like this. What are you doing with it here?" the refueling attendant asked.

"I've been tasked with mapping the Great Lakes shoreline. This is a research tool I use to search for major pollution sources."

"Working for the EPA?"

"There are several agencies, both here and internationally, who have an interest in what I am doing."

"Ever find any sunken ships with that thing? I've done some diving in the area myself. I never located anything worthwhile; bit of an amateur salvager. My father used to tell me stories about how the Purple Gang would buy whiskey in Canada and sail it around Mackinaw to Chicago, where they sold the Canadian whisky to the Capone organization. I've always thought that a few of those ships sank in the Great Lakes. One of these days, I'll find one."

Sam nodded to the refueling attendant, then made a mental note. After he returned the drone to the hangar, he mentioned the conversation to AMIE.

"One moment. Processing."

AMIE began researching lost ships and their cargo. "Sam, there are several thousand ships that have been reported missing in the Great Lakes. There is a ninety-seven percent probability that multiple ships have historical or salvage value. Do you wish me to pursue this venture?"

"As long as it doesn't detract from your primary function."

The first thing AMIE did was to plant stories in the local newspapers about bootlegging operations and historical accounts of various sunken ships.

AMIE instructed CAIO to use its sophisticated sonar equipment to map the entire shoreline of the Great Lakes and sent him out on his first mission.

* * *

Later that day, Sam took Helen to the hangar.

"Helen, I want you to meet AMIE."

"Who is Amie?"

Sam pointed to the row of computer stacks.

"AMIE, say hello to Helen."

"Hello Helen, it is good to meet you."

"Who said that?" Helen looked around for another person in the hangar.

"I'm sorry, dear. I didn't mean to startle you." Sam replied to his wife. "I programmed the computer with an audio interface to facilitate communication and coding."

"Sam, what is this?"

"AMIE is my assistant, my problem solver. She can assist you with any task. You just have to ask. AMIE, you may take instruction from Helen."

"Sam, you know I have no idea how these things work. I couldn't program a computer if my life depended on it."

The solemnity of that last comment struck a chord with Sam. "You don't need to program her, just ask her a question," Sam spoke softly.

"AMIE, can you print me a pattern for a Little Bo Peep? It's for a quilt I am making."

"What size do you require?"

"About seven inches tall will do nicely."

AMIE went online and selected a suitable pattern, then printed the various parts of the pattern, body, shoes, pantaloons, underskirt, apron, shepherds' staff, and hat, all to scale.

"This is incredible. But I am quite certain you didn't create this just to help with my quilting."

Sam kissed Helen on the forehead. "No dear. She's working on other problems."

Chapter 38

China

CHINA EVENTUALLY NOTICED THEY were missing a drone when it failed to return from its week-long assignment monitoring the western border.

A search team was assigned to track the flight path of the drone and determine exactly when it went missing. This proved more difficult than the Chinese military expected. There was no conclusive proof when it was stolen. The military knew someone had hacked their system because the drone continued to send spoofed footage from previous flights back to Chinese Intelligence long after it should have run low on fuel. The military searched the airspace and ground installations in Japan, Taiwan, South Korea, and the Ukraine first. These were the logical countries who had both the computer skills and the adversarial relationship to undertake such a treacherous act.

The search became painstakingly slow. The area that needed to be scanned was immense. China knew that whoever stole the drone would probably not keep it in the open. They would conceal it in a hanger somewhere where they could reverse engineer the technology.

China began monitoring the military chatter from around the globe to determine who might know about the missing drone, who had seen it flying overhead, and who was attempting to locate experts that could dismantle the technology and clone parts of the software. The embedded codes in the software that China installed in the event it needed to open a 'backdoor' to regain control of the drone no longer worked. This perplexed the Military. Never had any nation closed these doors on a Chinese technology. China put a team together to determine just how this might be accomplished and to prevent future technology theft.

Xiu Juan, from the Chinese Ministry of State Security, noticed the flash message regarding the theft of the Chinese drone.

"Damn. Who would steal another drone? Few countries have that technology." Xiu said to no one in particular. "I wonder."

Xiu picked up her phone and called Song Yi. "Yi? I want you to investigate Russia hacking techniques. Tell me if they have the capability to steal one of our drones."

"You suspect the Russians?" Yi's voice betrayed her surprise.

"A single conversation with a wise man is worth a month's study of books." Xiu quoted the proverb. "When I spoke with my Russian contact regarding the theft of the American drone, he never denied that they were behind the theft. I offered it was not us and he gave no reaction, no hint of surprise. Could the previous theft have been a failed Russian operation from the start? It was telling that a top Russian agent was involved. The Russians would not be so foolish to steal a second American drone, but they may be foolish enough to steal one of ours. Have our best computer 'intelligentized operations' technicians investigate Russia. Use satellite imagery to search for the missing drone on their soil and in their satellite states. And monitor Russian channels for chatter."

Chapter 40

Sam

EARLY THE NEXT MORNING, Helen packed her things and Sam loaded them into the car. Sam drove north through Cheboygan, then cut across on County Road Sixty-Six until he reached Lake Michigan. Turning south on M-119, he headed through the tunnel of trees past Harbor Springs and Petoskey until he reached M-37 and drove south to Brethren. Their circuitous trip took mostly state roads through scenic forests and small towns. It was a pleasant trip with his wife. Sam relished each moment.

The song Amie by Pure Prairie League played in the background on Sam's MP3 player.

> I can see why you think you belong to me
> I never tried to make you think
> Or let you see one thing for yourself
> But now you're off with someone else and I'm alone
> You see, I thought that I might keep you for my own
> Amie, what you wanna do?
> I think I could stay with you
> For a while, maybe longer if I do

Tom Parker was six-foot three-inches tall, a good five inches taller than his former classmate. He had kept most of his athletic build, though his gray hair betrayed his age. Tom eagerly greeted the pair as they pulled onto the gravel drive just as the sun reached its peak. "Great to see you again Sam," Tom grabbed Sam and gave him a hug, then turned to Helen. "Good to see you again. How long has it been?"

"Too long." Helen hugged Tom.

Tom and Sam brought the luggage into the house.

The place where Tom lived was in a secluded area a couple of miles outside town. Originally a hunter's cabin, Tom had worked hard the past six years, making additions and expanding it into a comfortable living space. There was a small pond to the north. To the south and west were dense woods. Tom had set up a small screened-in area for a garden. The screened fencing kept the critters away from the vegetables.

"I heard about the fire. Tough situation. You going to rebuild?"

"Eventually. Need to take care of a few things first."

"So, you really think the Russians would bother with a nobody from Michigan?"

"I know you think I'm paranoid, but I would rather be cautious than regretful."

"Helen is welcome to stay as long as you need. She will be good company. And who knows, perhaps she can teach me a new way to cook trout. Do you fish, Helen?"

"My dad used to take me when I was young. I haven't been fishing since," she tapped her lip, "I can't remember when."

"Sam. What kind of husband are you, anyway? Denying your wife the pleasure of fishing?"

Sam just shrugged his shoulders. He was not a fisherman.

After dinner, Sam kissed his wife goodbye. He kissed her as if it would be the last time, then he quickly got into the car and accidentally spun the tires on the gravel driveway as he backed out onto the two-lane road.

Tears glistened in the corner of his eye as he headed east to the lodge.

Chapter 39

Sam

THE THOUGHT THAT A MILITARY drone would become a useful tool came as a surprise to Sam. The spur-of-the-moment comment by the fuel attendant became the spark of inspiration that held a ray of hope.

Disguising the drone as a research tool helped, but Sam had a bigger problem: protecting the love of his life. He knew the Russians wanted him. Helen was of no use to the Russians except as a mechanism to hurt Sam or to manipulate him. Sam needed to find a solution that protected her.

Shipping her off to a relative was a risky proposition. If the Russians were smart enough to find him the first time, they would use any means necessary to achieve their goal. Helen was an active social media user. Her Facebook page was loaded with friends and family contacts. Contacts that could be used to locate and harm her.

Sam needed someone he could trust, someone with the necessary skills to protect Helen if it came down to that.

The only name that came to mind was his high school classmate, Tom Parker. Tom was a retired Michigan State Police trooper. He had the training necessary to act in hostile situations and lived far enough from

Northville that it was unlikely the Russians would discover him by accident.

When Tom retired, he moved up north to the small town of Brethren, close to Bear Creek, where Ernest Hemingway fished for trout in his teen years. Bear Creek is not as famous as the Two Hearted River in Michigan's Upper Peninsula, but it remained one of Hemmingway's favorites. Hemmingway used to say about the area, "Absolutely the best trout fishing in the country. No exaggeration." An avid fly-fisherman, Tom spent part of each day plying his craft in the peaceful, secluded waters of Northern Michigan.

Brethren was on the sunset side of Michigan. When Tom got the call from Sam, he was only too happy to help. Tom had followed the events of the drone incident and used to kid Pat and Sam about being terrorists when they met up at high school reunions.

Tom anticipated the arrival of his former classmate. It would be good to see Sam and Helen again. Life in Brethren was solitary since the death of his wife. It was a life Tom chose, but the loneliness sometimes bored into his soul.

* * *

Next, Sam had to explain the situation to his wife.

After dinner, he sat Helen down on the beach across from the lodge.

"Helen, we have to talk."

"This sounds serious."

"The Russians are back."

Helen gasped, placing her hand over her mouth. "How do you know?"

"I have been reluctant to say anything, but that is why we are up here. I am trying to stay off the grid, hoping that they can't track us." Sam hesitated. "There's more. They found our home in Northville. They destroyed it, burned it to the ground."

Helen covered her face with her hands and wept. "I never really believed that was an accident."

"No, it wasn't. This is going to be hard on both of us. I have asked a friend of mine to protect you. I will take you there tomorrow. You must let no one know where you are, no calls to family, no social media posts, nothing. As best you can, you must become invisible."

Helen turned to Sam, buried her face in his shoulder and wept.

Sam patted his wife on the back and kissed her cheek. He stroked her hair.

"I know. I wish with all my heart that we didn't have to go through this. I never wanted this for you. I need to keep you safe. It's me they want, not you. They will come for me. I can accept whatever death the Lord sends my way with all the pain, penalties, and sorrows, if only I know you are safe."

"Sam, you know I can't let you do this alone."

"You must."

"Are you certain they will come for you?"

"I'm uncertain of anything at this point. I have been preparing some options. AMIE is actually a Deep Learning computer programmed to study the situation. Hopefully, together, her cognitive computing capability, combined with my own, will be enough to survive the situation and bring about a peaceful resolution."

"Can't the FBI handle this?"

"The two agents we met with after the drone incident assured me they are doing everything possible. They offered to put us in a witness protection program. We can do that, if you want. It means permanently cutting ourselves off from all our relatives and friends. But you know me, I can't sit back and do nothing. I need to actively participate in our safety. That is why I'm taking you to Parker's tomorrow. You remember Tom. He's a good man; a former Michigan State Police trooper. He can handle himself and a gun if it comes to that. I'm not sure I would be much good in that situation. You know me and guns."

Helen lifted her face from his shoulder and smiled through her tears.

"There, that's what I wanted to see." Sam brushed the tear from Helen's cheek and kissed her soft lips.

Chapter 41

Sam

WHEN SAM ARRIVED BACK AT the lodge, he checked in with AMIE.

"What's the latest information?"

"Sam, may I have your SIM card?"

"Why? I thought my calls were encrypted."

"They are. I want to clone the card and use it to track the individuals that are attempting to track you. I will route all calls through my system and transfer the important ones to your phone via my secure Wi-Fi connection. In that way, I can screen the unwanted calls and scramble any attempt at surveillance. I can spoof your location sending the trackers to random locations around the country."

"Good idea."

Sam drove over to the hangar where AMIE now resided and pulled the SIM card out of his phone and inserted it into the memory slot on the workstation. AMIE immediately constructed a secure file folder to emulate the cell phone functions, then established a secure link to Sam's phone. In this way, Sam could talk to anyone, even someone on an unsecured phone, and the call would be invisible to anyone else.

Chapter 42

Sam

AMIE CALCULATED THE COST FOR this undertaking; housing for Sam and Helen, hangar rental, utilities, extra processing power, and data storage. She also factored in the prospect of hiring additional security. AMIE hacked into Sam's savings and brokerage accounts and determined that the expenses would consume a significant portion of his assets should the process continue for an extended period. She tapped into the blockchain environment and set up an efficient process for solving the computational problems involved with adding transaction records to Bitcoin's public ledger. This enabled AMIE to be paid in bitcoins, a cryptocurrency, for every transaction processed. The coins that were 'farmed' were used to purchase additional computational power and hard drives. Linking her new computers in parallel, Sam created a powerful supercomputer to expedite the calculations and house AMIE's ever growing intellect. This allowed her to multitask with no loss of efficiency.

When CAIO finished mapping the Great Lakes, AMIE established VGK Enterprises, LLC, to oversee the salvage operation. She analyzed the potential shipwreck locations provided by CAIO and compared them with public records and sent the locations of the most promising ships to salvage companies AMIE contracted through the LLC. These tasks were a sideline, albeit a profitable one, to her main purpose of protecting Sam and Helen.

Chapter 43

NEXT AMIE APPLIED FOR SALVAGE permits from the State Natural Resources Department and the Department of History, Arts, and Libraries, then hired a salvage firm to collect any valuables still intact within the hulls of the vessels CAIO had discovered. She assigned priorities to all the sunken relics.

Sam went with the salvage team, exploring the first ship off the coast of Alpena. He got caught up in the excitement the opportunity provided. Finding something of significance overcame his preoccupation with AMIE's investigation.

The arrangements AMIE made with the salvage operation were a fifty-fifty split of any salvage. She specifically excluded the contents of the captain's quarters. As it turned out, that was a strategically important exclusion.

Anchored above the location of the sunken ship, the captain confirmed the large object directly below using his onboard sonar.

"Alright men, here we go."

Accompanied by an underwater archaeologist from the state of Michigan, the three divers donned wetsuits as the water temperature at depth can be just above freezing even in July. Moving in the thick wetsuits was a chore. The four men wore rebreather systems that scrubbed the carbon dioxide from their breath and recycled the air, allowing them to dive deeper and stay down longer than they could with traditional open-circuit scuba gear. The dive team leader ran through the pre-dive checklist. A thumbs up from the team indicated that all were ready and they enter the water.

Twenty-five minutes later, an inflatable bag surfaced a few yards from the ship. A signal to the captain that the divers were all together, and the prompt for him to send out two safety divers along with a winch cable. A second bag popped up a few minutes later to signal that everything was secure and that the cable could be retracted.

After another twenty minutes passed, the team hauled themself back onto the deck, with no little effort, and began the laborious process of removing their equipment.

"Sir, we have cargo. It looks like cases of whiskey."

The captain turned to Sam.

"You were right. Probably Prohibition Era whiskey, judging from the age of the ship."

Sam nodded. He expected nothing less from AMIE and CAIO.

The hydraulic winch lifted the object and placed it on the deck of the ship. Sam's eyes widened as he looked at the 1920 vintage safe.

This was not the first safe the captain had come across in his salvage operation. He went to his cabin and brought out his stethoscope. Placing the resonator bell against the metal door, the captain slowly turned the dial to the right until he heard a click. He repeated the process, turning the dial to the left; then back to the right until the final click that unlocked the safe.

"The moment of truth." The captain slowly turned the handle and opened the safe. Inside he found a sealed, watertight captain's pouch that contained four stacks of bills packaged side by side measuring eleven inches tall, just over six inches wide and about fifteen inches long, wrapped in cellophane. The package contained ten-thousand 1920-vintage $10 bills and a ledger. AMIE's research of the ledger led her to historical IRS files linked to Al Capone and his Chicago organization. The sale of the ledger and the vintage currency provided ample funds to underwrite Sam's operation.

Two of the first five ships that were explored contained Prohibition Era Whiskey.

Chapter 44

Sam

THE PROCESS OF TRACKING the trackers became a priority. The attempts to track Sam's phone were being conducted in a sophisticated manner. AMIE developed an algorithm that would permit her to unravel the misdirection that had been complicating her search. She worked through the various spoofed locations intermixed with the normal overlay of spam phone calls. Determining the location where the trackers originated involved traversing down several blind alleys and rerouted connections.

Eventually, AMIE determined that the spoofed information she had been sending from Sam's phone was being relayed to a location in Shelby Township in Southeast Michigan. AMIE dispatched CAIO to surveil the area. Using the reconnaissance capabilities of the drone, AMIE analyzed the surrounding area. She uploaded scans of visual images of the pedestrians roaming the streets, then hacked into the traffic cameras, storefront security cameras and even the network of police cooperation agreements with various home security cameras. Using the facial recognition software she had procured earlier; AMIE compared the individuals to a database of suspects. The software identified a familiar face, Dmitri Peskov. Clearly, the tracking team reported to Peskov.

AMIE instructed CAIO to lock onto Dmitri and track his moves. He entered an office building on the corner of Van Dyke and Twenty-Four Mile Road in the downtown district. CAIO continued to monitor the location and later that evening tracked Dmitri leaving the office complex and driving to an apartment about a half mile away. CAIO transmitted the information.

AMIE sent an encrypted photo to Sam's phone with the name Dmitri Peskov. She sent a file with his current address in Michigan and notified Sam that she had confirmation that this was the man tracking him. She also sent the information to Agents Cooper and Patton.

This came as no surprise to Sam. He had long feared that someone associated with Vasili would come after him. He now had a face and a location. It wouldn't be long before the man in the photo would locate him. The time arrived for Sam to make additional plans.

W. M. J. KREUCHER

Chapter 45

Dmitri

OVER THE NEXT SEVERAL DAYS, seven distinct assets, counting Dmitri, entered the office complex at the corner of Van Dyke and Twenty-Four Mile Road at various times. Inside, on the second floor, was the FSB tactical office. The assets searched for Sam and James, tracking down the various leads. The leads sent by AMIE convinced the team that Sam was on the run traveling around the country. James presented a unique problem. Though the team previously identified over a hundred individuals matching the name James O'Connor, none seemed to match the profile Evgeny developed. O'Connor seemed to have vanished from the grid, and that made him a prime suspect in Evgeny's mind.

The assets provided daily updates to Dmitri, who entered the building at precisely eight-fifty-nine each morning. In his hand, he always held a cup of Jardin espresso. Dmitri never could acquire a taste for Caffè Americano.

"Today our friend is in Jupiter, Florida. He seems to be the nervous type, never staying in one place more than a single night."

"Can you blame him? He must think we are going to hold him to account for losing our comrade, Vasili. But I assure you, we are not out to kill him. I only want to know how our friend died." Dmitri smiled as he sipped his espresso. He thumbed through the Shamrock yearbook that sat on the table.

The men in the room smirked. They knew Dmitri's reputation.

"We need not chase him around the country. We must convince our friend to come to us. Is his wife with him?"

"Comrade, we are uncertain."

"Well, get certain. I want to know by tomorrow where she is."

The assets looked at each other. There was a collective gulp. The nervous Mikhailov blinked twice.

"What's this?" Dmitri asked, holding up the book.

"It's Mr. Kennedy's high school yearbook. We picked it up from his home before the unfortunate accident. We thought it might prove useful." Eduard grinned.

Dmitri thumbed through the yearbook, then identified Sam's photo. "How young he looks, not at all like a trained killer. But those are the most effective. They hide in plain sight."

Dmitri paged forward and looked for the photo of James O'Connor. He found none. The only O'Connor listed in the yearbook was Patrick.

"Did you notice the photo of Patrick O'Connor?"

"Nyet. Do you know him?"

Idiots, why is everyone who works for me an idiot? Dmitri thought.

"Perhaps the reason we cannot find James O'Connor is that he uses his middle name?"

Dmitri handed the book to Eduard, tapping on the photograph.

The men had failed to locate O'Connor, largely because they were searching for the wrong man.

"We will update our search immediately." Eduard looked at Major Andrej Novikov, the computer technician on loan from the Red Army, who put his head down and began typing on his keyboard.

The room the assets occupied was a specially prepared room-in-a-room with no windows and only a single door. The space was constructed to shield outsiders from prying. Once inside the room, no one could see, hear, or otherwise know what the men inside were doing. This was Dmitri's safe space.

* * *

Once outside the room, however, there was no hiding from the prying eyes of AMIE and CAIO. They tracked every move each of the Russians made. This was no small task as first AMIE had to rule out those exiting the building who were not a threat. Each person who came out of the office complex had to be tracked, identified, and assessed. Individuals were compared against drivers' license pictures, passport photos, and visa requests.

Several individuals were undocumented. AMIE kept these individuals in a separate file. She identified seven men with connections to Russia. These she prioritized. It took several computational hours to determine that six of the men, including Dmitri Peskov, had ties to the FSB. The seventh was identified as a computer technician who had a commission in the Red Army. Eventually, she identified Eduard Orlov and Robert Mikhailov from the dossiers she unearthed at the FSB.

These two men posed a significant risk as their training regime included various Russian martial arts, including SAMBO (self-defense without weapons), SYSTEMA (the system), and ARB (Army hand-to-hand combat). Their past operations included assassinations and extractions. Robert Mikhailov was also a trained chemist.

In the wee hours of the morning, AMIE compiled a dossier on Orlov, Mikhailov, and each of the other four Russians. She already had a dossier on Peskov. The information contained their real names, the names on their passports, and the information in their visas. She determined that falsifying this information was a federal offense. Included in her dossier was the location of the tactical operating center in Shelby Township and the apartments that were rented to house the men.

AMIE sent the information to the FBI in care of Agents Cooper and Patton.

Chapter 46

FBI

"COOP, DID YOU READ THE ENCRYPTED email from Special Agent AMIE?"

"You know, I never heard of her until the recent string of emails. We have been getting a lot of intelligence from her lately. I hope it's trustworthy. I haven't had time to check the company mail today. Anything important in the email?"

"It seems there are six Russian FSB agents operating at a clandestine location in Southeastern Michigan, plus a Red Army Major. Do you think these are the agents who are searching for our Mr. Kennedy?"

"There can't be two sets of agents operating in Michigan. We better check it out."

"Should we contact the local office and have them run a check?"

"Alright. We can notify Mr. Kennedy when we get something concrete."

* * *

In the morning, two agents from the FBI's Detroit field office were dispatched to Shelby Township. They drove around the block where the office was located, then parked their vehicle two blocks away. The agents walked down the street and entered Militello's Bakery near the corner of Twenty-Four Mile Road and Van Dyke at seven fifteen. They purchased two cups of coffee and each agent selected a pastry. Then the men stood in the window and watched the building across the street. After observing several individuals enter the target building, the agents gulped the last sips of coffee and discarded the cups in the trash before exiting the bakery.

The FBI agents walked outside and crossed Van Dyke. Carefully taking out his phone, Agent Wieder nonchalantly snapped a photograph of the license plate of each of the vehicles in the parking lot and sent the photos to the field office for identification. Afterwards, he continued walking with his partner through the parking lot, exiting at the far end.

The onsite agents conferred with Agents Cooper and Patton, who requested a closer look at the vehicles. The two FBI agents walked back into the parking lot and peered inside the first vehicle they came across. A text came back from the Detroit Field office identifying the registered owners of the vehicles in the parking lot.

Agents Crites and Wieder walked over to the van with the word Consul clearly printed on the license plate.

"Do I see drugs in the center console?" Special Agent Crites said, looking at his partner.

"You know, that looks suspicious. We now have probable cause." Special Agent Wieder winked at his partner.

Special Agent Crites opened the FBI app on his phone and tapped on the vehicle icon. After a few more taps, he photographed the vehicle identification number, then waited for the lock/unlock button to turn green. When he pressed the button, the doors of the van unlocked.

Entering the van, Special Agent Crites opened the glove box and examined its contents. Taking out the vehicle registration, he photographed it, then showed it to his partner.

"Russian Consulate."

"No surprise, the license plate told us that. The boys in legal are not going to like this."

"Screw them. We need to find out what they are up to way out here in the boonies."

Special Agent Wieder entered the back seat and picked up a book. "What's this?"

He showed the hardcovered book to his partner.

"High school yearbook?"

"Yes, but who's?"

"Only one way to find out." Special Agent Crites nodded with his head towards the book.

Wieder opened the blue-gray covered nineteen-hundred sixty-nine edition of the Shamrock yearbook. Inside the front cover were several acknowledgements from classmates. All of them were addressed 'to Sam.' Agent Wieder thumbed through the pages, stopping at page forty. In the top left corner of the page was a photo with a caption 'Sam Kennedy.'

"Why would they have his high school yearbook?"

Wieder shrugged his shoulders. "Likely starting point for 'known accomplices?' We need to notify Agents Cooper and Patton right away. They're going to have to find Sam and let him know he's in trouble before the trouble finds him."

* * *

Dmitri drove past the building and was about to turn into the parking lot when he spotted two suspicious men. He could spot an FBI agent a mile away. Dmitri continued driving south on Van Dyke. Convinced he was not being followed, Dmitri pulled into the parking lot of Trinity Lutheran church and called his agents.

"We have visitors."

A few minutes later, Eduard called Dmitri back. "G-men."

"We will have to be careful. We're being watched."

Chapter 47

DMITRI PULLED THE SIM CARD and the micro-SD memory card from his phone and slipped them into his pocket. He logged out of each account on his phone and removed all the apps he had installed, then did a factory reset on the phone. Dmitri removed the case and wiped the phone of all fingerprints. Opening the door, Dmitri slipped the phone under the car directly behind the front wheel, then he backed out of the parking space. Now his clandestine field training kicked in.

Dmitri drove around Southeastern Michigan for the next ten hours. He stopped at banks and walked inside. Then stopped at various office complexes and went inside. He went to shopping malls, parks, restaurants, and college campuses. Each time, he waited an appropriate amount of time until he could ascertain if he was being observed.

Convinced he was not being followed, he returned to his apartment and logged onto his computer. He ordered a new Taiga phone from Russia and had it express shipped through a Canadian company to a post office box in Madison Heights. The Russian company specifically modified the android operating system on the phone to run in tandem with InfoWatch firmware to make the phone surveillance proof.

The next evening, Dmitri retrieved his new phone.

Dmitri connected the phone to his computer and uploaded FSB encryption software and other operational apps.

Because AMIE had earlier hacked into Dmitri's computer, she was able to monitor all of Dmitri's keystrokes. Using the GoldenHelper app she borrowed from China, AMIE sent an infected GIF through Dmitri's computer and installed the ForcedEntry app she had borrowed from the Israeli Ministry of Defense on Dmitri's new phone, setting up a backdoor. In this way, she maintained full access to its location, text information, and phone calls. She deleted the GIF after infecting the phone, leaving no trace that the phone had been infected.

After rebooting his phone, Dmitri called Viktor Matviyenko, his right-hand man coordinating 'Operation Reprisal'.

Dmitri spoke only a single word into the phone, "Gorbachev", then he hung up.

Viktor understood the code word. The operation had been compromised. He communicated the information to the rest of the team and implemented a prearranged operational plan. No longer would Dmitri come into the office for his daily briefing. The team would continue to work in the secure office, but all communication with Dmitri would occur at locations that changed daily. Each meeting would establish the location and time of the next meeting.

Dmitri was taking no chances that the American government would interfere with his plans.

Chapter 48

AGENTS COOPER AND PATTON contacted Sam and passed along the information that Special Agent Crites and Wieder provided, sketchy as it was.

"You don't sound surprised." Cooper said.

"Not really. This has been my nightmare ever since that day in the field when Vasili ..." Sam's voice trailed off.

"We will send someone to keep you safe. Just where are you?"

Sam hesitated. He really didn't know the last location AMIE had passed along to the men following him and was reluctant to provide his actual location, fearing the FBI phones might be compromised.

"I'll get back to you on that. I'm not in harm's way at the moment."

"Mr. Kennedy, you are in harm's way, whether or not you realize it. We need to send some federal marshals."

"Okay. I'm leaving now and will text you with my location tonight." Sam hung up the phone and went to see AMIE.

"Now, what do we do? Do you have a plan?"

"Yes, Sam. I have swapped your phone's mobile subscriber identity with that of a traveling salesman. He is headed towards California as we speak. That should keep the Russians occupied for the moment."

"Alright, but we need a more permanent solution. These people will not stop until I'm dead."

"I will not let that happen, Sam. I am working on a long-term resolution."

AMIE finished updating the dossier on Niklas Sussman aka Dmitri Peskov and forwarded it to Agents Cooper and Patton. The dossier contained his current position as head of the FSB, his life's story, his photograph, a complete list of his aliases, his present location in the United States, and the number of the new phone Dmitri just ordered.

The two agents investigated the findings. Agent Cooper sent a request to the CIA, who used their tracking tools to locate Dmitri. The CIA confirmed some of the information in the dossier, including Dmitri's current position as head of the FSB. However, the last known contact information on the suspect led them to determine Dmitri was still in Russia. The CIA agents couldn't even hack into the phone number provided in the dossier and they were unaware their own boss had met with Dmitri on US soil just a few weeks earlier. Because they concluded Dmitri was in Russia, they did not send the information up the chain of command. Instead, the CIA agents reported back to the FBI that they were mistaken and that Peskov posed no immediate treat on American soil.

Confused by the contradictory information between what the CIA concluded and the anonymous information, Agents Cooper and Patton initiated extradition proceedings, anyway.

The process for extraditing a Russian citizen was long and complex. It involved extraditing the person to Saudi Arabia and then to the United States. Processing the paperwork through the Department of Justice for a warrant and extradition request meant it needed to be coordinated through the State Department, and that meant time, time that the FBI did not think they had. The initial contact with the Saudi Arabian Embassy through back channels reported that their Russian contacts claimed Dmitri was living a peaceful, retired life in a Moscow suburb.

Chapter 49

AN ALERT FLASHED IN THE CORNER of Fancy Bear's monitor as he played Galaga.

"You found me a breadcrumb, good girl," Evgeny Naumov - AKA Fancy Bear said to his beloved companion. This wasn't the first breadcrumb the computer had found. Evgeny hoped this one would prove more useful than those in the past.

The credit card of Helen Kennedy had been used at Two Sisters Quilt shop in Manistee, Michigan.

Evgeny tapped on the keyboard, uploading all the names of her relatives and friends he had collected from social media. This was an exercise he had performed many times before. Nothing turned up in the local area. Next, Evgeny uploaded the names from the nineteen hundred sixty-nine edition of the Shamrock yearbook. He had found a digital version online after a tip from Victor. The optical character reader function translated the names and placed them in a file. The Asymmetry computer searched the surrounding area for Sam's classmates. Tom Parker's name popped up in Brethren, Michigan, a short twenty-four miles from where the credit card was used.

"Bingo" shouted Evgeny as he raised his hands in joy. "Evgeny, you've done it again."

* * *

The next morning at the appointed time, Viktor Matviyenko met Dmitri on the heron's view benches in Holland Pond Park in Macomb County. The benches sat across the wetland from the heronry where great blue heron's nested in the trees.

"We have located her."

"Mrs. Kennedy?"

"Yes, Sir. She used her credit card in a quilt shop in Manistee in the northwest corner of Michigan. Our computer team located a classmate of Mr. Kennedy in the surrounding area. We have two men on route as we speak. I will join them shortly."

"Excellent work. She is not to be harmed, at least for the moment. Now we will see if Mr. Kennedy knows how to play ball."

It didn't take long for the Russians to reach the small town of Brethren. Describing Brethren as a small town did a disservice to small towns. The town didn't even have traffic light, only a four-way stop at the crossroad of the two major streets in what would otherwise be the center of town. With a population of four hundred, everyone knew everyone. Except during deer season when hunters invaded the entire northern part of the state. Throughout firearm season, the sound of gunfire was so prevalent that no one noticed or turned their heads.

* * *

Helen felt safe in the area and with Tom. He was tall, a retired Michigan State Police trooper, and knew how to handle guns. Tom was an avid hunter. His prey changed with the season, which always ended up on his dinner table. Tom lived in a densely wooded area just outside town on Swihart Road. There were only two other houses on that mile stretch of road. Tom's neighbors were wild turkey, deer, bear, and the occasional coyote. World class trout and salmon fishing spots dotted the area along the Manistee River, a half mile south of his cabin.

When the Russians drove through the area, they stopped at Traks Bar and Grill to get the local gossip. It was a quiet, rustic place frequented by locals and popular with the hunters. Nothing fancy. The tongue-in-groove knotty pine walls accented the wood bar and the black wrought-iron chairs with matching vinyl seat cushions. The locals were friendly, but didn't offer information to strangers about any of their neighbors. They kept to themselves and protected their own.

Viktor and his two accomplices rented a small hunter's cabin and talked mostly about hunting and fishing. The conversation was generic. It was impossible for anyone to tell if their exploits were in the local area or back home in Russia. They ate at Traks every night for a week.

Then it happened. Tom showed up on Friday night for the fish fry. It was the best in the area, and Tom loved fish.

Viktor recognized Tom from the reconnaissance dossier that had been prepared for him. He listened intently to the conversation until he heard someone call out Tom's name.

The three Russians left the bar and waited in the parking lot for their prey to finish dining.

Tom came out of the bar with several friends. They spoke for a few minutes outside, under the lights in front of the bar. Tom paid little attention to the men sitting in a car near the edge of High Bridge Road. He got into his car and headed south, then made a left turn at the first intersection, then another left onto Swihart. The Russians followed at a distance and turned off their headlights before making the last turn.

* * *

The sound of crunching gravel in the driveway later that night caused Tom's ears to perk.

"Who could that be at this hour?"

Helen looked up from her quilting and shrugged her shoulders. "I'm sure I don't know anyone around here."

Tom put a finger to his lips, then motioned for Helen to follow him. He grabbed his phone, and they each picked up a 'go bag' positioned at the back door and exited. Tom quietly shut the door, and the pair disappeared into the dark forest behind the cabin.

Tom took up a position in a deer blind and opened the app for the front door camera, being careful to shield the glow of the phone from prying eyes.

He showed Helen the image of three men wearing all black.

Helen shook her head.

The sharp rap of knuckles on the wood door echoed through the forest. A nearby doe picked up her ears to listen.

After a few minutes, Tom could see the shadows of two men circling the house, one clockwise, the other counter-clockwise. They stopped to peer into each window. One man pulled something from his coat pocket and, within a few seconds, the back door opened. The two shadows disappeared into Tom's cabin.

Twenty-seven minutes later, the sound of tires on the gravel gave the all-clear signal. Tom could not be sure the house was empty.

"We don't need to speculate what that was about. They've found us."

Helen's entire body tightened reflexively. "What do we do now?"

"Well, if they were doing what I think they were doing, we can't go back inside. It would take too long for me to locate all the surveillance gear that now resides in my cabin. Come on."

Helen followed Tom as he walked deeper into the forest. After about a half-mile walk, Tom mounted his ATV, strategically placed for just this occasion. "I have some friends who have a cabin a couple of miles from here. They're away, so we can stay there for the time being."

* * *

Tom found the key to the cabin above the inside doorjamb of the outhouse. He let Helen into the cabin.

"We should be safe here." His voice provided no comfort.

"How did they find us?"

"I don't know—but for the time being, I'm afraid you can't go into town. We have to assume they know your face. I'm just not sure if they know mine. We'll have to chance it. We'll need groceries. I'll call a friend and have her bring some things in the morning."

"Can I call Sam? I want to make sure he's still safe."

"Here, use my phone. They may have a trace on yours."

Helen's face betrayed her concern. Just the day before, she had called a friend to tell her she was in Northern Michigan.

"Sam?"

"Helen? It's good to hear your voice. How are you? Tom keeping you safe?"

"I'm safe. Tom is too, for now."

"Why? What's happened?"

"They found us."

Sam hesitated before responding. "I'm so sorry for getting you involved in this."

"It's not your fault, dear. I know you had to kill that Russian fella. If you hadn't, he would have surely killed you. And Tom is taking good care of me. I won't tell you where we are, but for now, we are both safe."

"That's good. I'll secure Tom's phone so it can't be traced."

"I'll tell him. And is my phone secure?"

"Yes, I did that some time ago."

Helen exhaled a sigh of relief.

* * *

In the morning, Tom contacted his friend. "Abbie, it's Tom. I need you to do me a favor."

"Sure, Darlin, anything for you." Abbie had been sweet on Tom ever since he retired in Brethren.

"Can you pick up a few groceries? I can text you a list. I'm staying at the Rawski place for a few days while I redo the bathroom in my cabin. I've been meaning to get to that ever since I moved here."

"Sure, but it will be late before I get to it. I'm working today till six."

"No worries."

Tom hung up the phone and texted a list of staples that he needed.

Helen went into the refrigerator and pulled out the fixings for scrambled eggs. "Eggs okay this morning, Tom?"

"Sure. I'll make the coffee."

"Can you make some tea for me, please?"

"I'll see what I can find."

"Tom, I'm worried."

"To tell the truth, so am I."

"Do you think you are a good enough shot to kill those men?"

"Kill them? I don't know. We don't know for sure how many of them there are. We saw three, but there could be others."

"But what if we had information on them, tracked their whereabouts, that sort of thing?"

"I suppose. Do you want me to get the FBI involved? I still have some friends at the State Police that owe me a favor."

"From what Sam says, those people may not have the resources to locate all of them fast enough."

"He may be right. If they are KGB, we could be in real danger."

"I was thinking. Sam's pretty good with computers. He's been playing with this fancy computer that can talk to him. Perhaps we could get that thing to track these men."

"That would take some fancy computing. Can Sam do that?"

"I don't know. But it's be worth a try. I'll ask him. Do you think it would be possible for you to go get my quilting supplies? I'd like to keep my hands busy so my mind doesn't spin any ..."

"I know what you mean. I'm edgy myself. Let me give some thought as to how I might sneak back into the cabin. But first we need to get out of this cabin. You up for some fishing today?" Tom always thought better when he was fishing.

"That's an excellent idea."

After breakfast, Tom packed up two sets of waders, a couple of fly-casting rods and other gear. Helen packed a lunch, and they got into Tom's car and headed to Bear Creek.

* * *

At precisely six-thirty, Abbie knocked on the door of the Rawski place. Tom let his friend into the cabin.

"I brought you the things you wanted. Oh, I didn't know you had company. Hi, I'm Abbie." Abbie had dressed up, expecting to be alone with Tom and was surprised to find another woman in the cabin. She didn't offer a hand.

Helen stood up and responded to the look of surprise on Abbie's face. "Hi, I'm Helen. Please to meet you and thank you for running this errand." Helen held out her hand, which Abbie accepted.

"My pleasure. Tom? What's going on?" Still confused by the situation she found herself in, Abbie turned to Tom.

"It's not what you think. Helen is the wife of a high school classmate. She's staying with me for a few weeks while he gets some things settled. I can't really go into it. Please don't say anything in town. You know how rumors start in Brethren. You just have to trust me that this is all on the up and up."

"Then you're not remodeling?"

"No."

The confused look on Abbie's face told Tom and Helen she wasn't buying the story.

"Then why are you staying here? Why can't you go home?"

"I just can't. You have to believe me. I can't go into it now. I'll explain it all later."

Abbie took that as her cue. It was time for her to depart.

"That was awkward. Is she your girl?" Helen asked.

"No, but she wants to be. I've lived alone now for so long I don't know if I could live with another person again."

"I know what you mean. If something ever happened to Sam, I don't think I could remarry. Sam jokes with me about it, but I just don't think I could start over again." A tear glistened on Helen's cheek.

* * *

Abbie Hochhauser was a stocky Jewish woman living in a Christian community. She no longer practiced her faith ever since the premature death of her husband ten years earlier. She moved from New York to the remote community of Brethren a year after her husband passed.

Abbie walked into Traks, sat at the bar and ordered a cosmopolitan. "Can you believe that Tom Parker?"

"What's he done now?" The bartender asked, bringing Abbie her drink. His voice betrayed his lack of interest.

"He's shacking up with some bimbo at the Rawski place. And what's worse, she's the wife of a friend."

At this, every ear in the place turned to the conversation at the bar, including those of the three strangers sitting at the table in the corner.

"Tom isn't the type to do something like that. I don't believe it."

"Neither would I if I didn't see it with my own two eyes. I just came from the house."

"You're overreacting. I'm certain there's some other explanation."

Abbie did not answer. She just took a long sip from her Cosmo.

* * *

The three strangers got up, paid their tab, left a generous tip, and walked out the door. Before exiting, they stopped at the phone in the lobby and paged through the phone book, looking for an address.

"I thought we were going to have to go door to door to find those two. Now they have been gifted to us by a jealous girlfriend." Viktor chuckled.

The trio got into the car and drove to the address. The lights were on, so they drove past and stopped a quarter mile north. Eduard opened the trunk and pulled out his sniper rifle and a second rifle for Robert. They screwed on the silencers and cocked their weapons.

Walking through the woods, Eduard took up a position north of the cabin. He had a view of the kitchen window. Robert took the southern position opposite one of the bedroom windows. Viktor camped across the street with a view of the living room and the front door.

* * *

Tom was nursing a beer and watching Magnum PI. Helen was working on her Bo Peep quilt, which Tom had surreptitiously retrieved that afternoon after the fishing trip. She had just finished her tea when Tom got up from his Lazy-boy.

"I think I'm going to hit the sack." He picked up his empty bottle.

"You finished?"

"Yes Tom, I'm going to bed too." She put down her quilting. "But first, I want to call Sam."

Tom walked into the kitchen and loaded Helen's cup and saucer into the dishwasher, then added the soap and set the dishwasher to turn on after a two-hour delay.

Helen picked up her phone and dialed.

Sam answered the call. "Helen, how are you?"

"I'm fine, just wanted to hear a familiar voice. I wanted to talk to you about that computer you showed me the other day."

"You sure you're okay? You sound a bit on edge? Still worried about ..."

The tinkling of glass preceded the thud of Tom's body hitting the floor. A pool of crimson seeped onto the cream-colored linoleum below Tom's head.

Hearing the noise, Helen walked into the kitchen. She screamed.

Just then, the door of the cabin burst open, and three foreigners rushed inside. Viktor grabbed the phone from Helen's hand. Robert grabbed Helen and clamped his hand over her mouth. He blinked twice as he glanced at Victor. Waiting for what might come next.

Viktor looked at the phone and realized Helen was speaking with Sam. "I will not bother you with my name. It is unimportant. Just know that if you ever want to see this woman again, you must meet us. We will call tomorrow with a time and a place. I need not explain what will happen if you fail."

Stunned by the sudden change in events, Sam did not answer.

Viktor hit the end call key on the phone and placed it in his pocket.

Chapter 50

THE SITUATION WAS DESPERATE. Panicked by the call from his wife, Sam phoned AMIE.

"I just got a call ..." the pace of his voice confirmed his agitation.

"Yes, Sam, I am aware of the situation. I monitored the call. Dmitri will no doubt take her to a location near his office or perhaps his apartment. He will call you to arrange a meeting. The meeting place will be in a remote location. Somewhere where he will feel safe and can control the situation. It is indeterminable if he will have Helen with him."

"AMIE, I can't lose her. Find Helen and get her to safety. Call Tom, find out where he is. Call the state police, the FBI ..."

"Sam, I know you do not want to hear this, but Dmitri will not harm Helen, at least not until he has you. He is setting a trap, and Helen is the bait. She will be kept alive until you are in his clutches. He is ruthless, but he knows how to leverage a situation. Once he has you, however; that is another matter. He will have no further use for Helen and there is a ninety-eight-point seven percent probability he will kill both of you."

"Unless you give me a better option. I have no choice but to do what he asks no matter how small the probability that my Helen will live."

"Can you give me some time to consider options?"

"AMIE, the timing is out of my control. Do what you can."

Sam hung up the phone. His heart pounded in his chest as he grabbed the suitcase and threw it on the bed. Arms full of clothes were tossed into the open case. When everything was cleared out of the room, Sam raced down the stairs of the lodge and threw the room key at the clerk.

"Send me the bill," he shouted before exiting the main doors. He climbed into his car and pointed it towards Brethren.

This is a mistake, he thought. *I don't have a plan; I don't have a place to stay.*

Sam turned the car around and headed to Alpena. Entering the hangar where CAIO stood, Sam reinstalled the eight AR-1 missiles to CAIO's fuselage. He now had the capability of taking out a convoy of armored vehicles.

Sam lost his home; his wife had been kidnapped, again, and a killer was on his trail. The thought of losing his wife stuck in his throat as he finished his task. He wiped the tears from his eyes.

Sam spoke with his computer, "AMIE? I want you to dispatch CAIO. Have him locate Helen. I don't want him discharging the weapons unless you are one-hundred percent certain she is safe." Sam opened the door of the hangar and watched as CAIO taxied to the runway. Closing the hangar door, Sam exited and got into his car, pointing it toward Brethren.

It was after four in the morning when Sam turned south onto High Bridge Road into Brethren. Sam pulled into the parking lot of the Manistee Outpost motel and just sat there. The cramps in his hands from squeezing the wheel for so long made it difficult to release their hold. Sam took a deep breath and forced his hands to open, then he got out of the car and walked inside. He paid cash for one night.

When he got inside his room, he called Agent Cooper.

"They have kidnapped my wife. I don't know where they are taking her."

"Mr. Kennedy? Is that you? Where are you and who kidnapped your wife?"

"I'm in a motel just south of Brethren. I was talking to Helen just after ten and a Russian voice came on the line and told me if I ever wanted to see my wife again, I had to do exactly what they said."

"And what was that?"

"That's just it, they didn't say. All they said was that they would call me and tell me where to meet them and that if I didn't show up, they would kill Helen." Sam's voice grew more agitated as the conversation continued. *This is pointless*, he thought.

"Was Helen with you when she was kidnapped?"

"No, she was with a friend, Tom Parker. He's a retired state trooper. Tom lives in Brethren in the northwest corner of the state?"

"Which state?"

"Michigan." Sam almost shouted into the phone.

"We will contact Mr. Parker and put out an all-points-bulletin. You don't happen to know the type of car he drives?"

"No" Sam's voice grew forlorn.

"No worries, we will place a tracer on Helen's phone, that is, if she still has it with her."

"I'm sure she does, or at least the Russians have it. They are going to use it to contact me."

"Good, then we will know where they are. I can monitor your phone as well. No sense taking chances."

Sam put the phone down and collapsed on the bed.

Chapter 51

AMIE SENT A SIGNAL TO REACTIVATE the GPS on Helen's phone and dispatched CAIO to search the surrounding area.

With a clear signal, CAIO turned south, tracking the phone. Traveling two-point-five kilometers behind, CAIO followed two vehicles speeding south on I-75. He relayed the position to AMIE.

Eventually, the vehicles stopped at a rest area near mile marker one-fifty-eight. In the glow of the streetlights illuminating the rest area, CAIO monitored four individuals exiting the two vehicles and entering a building. She sent a message to AMIE. "The vehicles are empty. Am I authorized to destroy them?"

AMIE replied, "Request denied. Our orders are to destroy all the assailants only if we can guarantee that Helen is safe from harm. Based on the information available, we cannot make that guarantee."

CAIO continued to monitor the situation.

Fifteen minutes later, all four individuals exited the building and returned to the vehicles. CAIO relayed the updated information.

AMIE instructed CAIO to continue monitoring.

CAIO updated the status when the vehicles reentered southbound traffic. Two hours later, CAIO observed four individuals exiting the vehicles and entering an apartment in Shelby Township. CAIO dutifully notified AMIE.

AMIE instructed CAIO to take up a surveillance position and continue monitoring the situation. There was no point attacking the apartment, the risk of civilian casualties was too great.

Chapter 52

DMITRI'S PATIENCE WAS RUNNING out. Even at the best of times, he was not a patient man. Now, with his goal close at hand, his thirst for retribution grew with each passing moment. He had not slept well that night, nor the night before. The vodka he consumed caused his heart to beat irregularly. The memory of Vasili haunted him in his dreams. No, not dreams, nightmares. He wanted the man who killed Vasili with every fiber of his being.

Early that morning, he texted Victor. "Are you near?"

The vibration of the phone startled Victor. Still groggy from only a few hours' sleep, he texted back. "Da."

"Good. Keep her close. I will contact our friend and make arrangements this evening. Bring me the woman's phone."

* * *

An incoming call startled Sam awake. He picked up his phone, still in a daze from his slumber.

"Helen? Is that you?"

"No, Mr. Kennedy. It is not your wife."

Sam's throat tightened. "Who is this?"

"My name does not matter. Let us just say that I am a friend of Vasili. He was like a son to me and you took him from me. Now I must take something from you."

"No, wait. Please."

"Begging? That is not becoming. You are clearly not a trained asset. I wonder just how you killed my dear Vasili."

"That's a long story." Sam regained his wits as the rush of adrenaline pushed away the fog of sleep from his mind.

"Perhaps you can tell me when I see you. You have one hour. I will be at the Centennial Cemetery off Clark Road in New Haven, Michigan."

"I can't get back to Michigan in an hour. I'm in California." Sam replied, recalling where AMIE said his phone signal originated from. "I don't have sufficient funds to fly, so I have to drive. You will recall your people hacked into my bank accounts and stole all my money after you burned down my home." Sam knew AMIE had prevented the incursion. He was counting on the fact that his adversary hadn't been made aware of the failure yet.

"Oh, yes. I forgot. My memory isn't what it used to be. Alright, I will call you tomorrow with a new location. I suggest you drive fast."

Sam hung up the phone and paced around the small motel room. It wasn't in him to sit idle while danger surrounded his wife. He called AMIE.

"What can you tell me? Do you have a plan?"

"Working on it. There are many variables to consider. I have not been able to reach Mr. Parker. His phone is turned off. I have reactivated it, but he is not answering my calls and the phone is not at his home. I will continue to monitor the situation and alert you when something develops."

"That doesn't sound right. Tom wouldn't leave Helen. Perhaps you should send CAIO to search the area."

"If that is your wish. Dmitri is in Shelby Township. Helen is in a nearby apartment with three others. I have dispatched CAIO to surveil the area in order to ascertain when and if Helen is moved. If you want me to issue a change in his orders, I can do that."

"No, Tom can take care of himself. On second thought, can you send the location information for Tom's phone to the State Police? Perhaps they can find him. And keep monitoring Helen. Send me her location. Perhaps between the two of us, we can rescue her."

Sam considered the possibility of notifying the FBI and giving them Helen's location. He quickly discarded the idea, fearing the prospect that his wife might be hurt in the crossfire that might result when the Bureau stormed the apartment. Sam packed the car and headed for the location AMIE sent.

Chapter 53

HELEN WAS IN SHELBY TOWNSHIP locked in the spare bedroom in Victor's apartment.

"You may scream if you like. It will be the last words you will ever issue. It's up to you."

"Can I call Sam?"

"Perhaps we will allow you to talk with him tomorrow. Today, he is traveling. When he arrives, we will arrange a trade, your life for his."

Shock at the bluntness of the last comment washed over Helen's face. She understood the situation. Her faith that Sam had come through for her the last time had somehow kept her spirits up. Now doubt crept in. No longer could she conceive of a rescue that would succeed against such men. Sam was smart, but could he defeat so many men? An entire country aligned against him? And where were those stupid FBI people? Why didn't they recognize the threat and neutralize it? Helen's mind struggled against the harshness of the reality.

Periodically, someone would bring in a plate of food. Helen barely touched it. She drank the tea they brought and ran her fingers over her white rosary beads, a gift from her mother on her First Communion, reciting the prayers she and Sam had said together on so many occasions. There was comfort in the prayers. It brought peace to her thoughts.

In the other room, Helen could hear the hushed voices of two or three men, all with Russian accents. This kidnapping was unlike the previous one. This time, Helen did not have a companion. Now she could hear the voices of her captors. Helen could not always distinguish the construct of the plan that was discussed mostly in Russian, but the tone of the voices she overheard brought tears to her eyes.

As the hours passed, the voices became more strident, impatient. They seemed to be waiting for something or someone. Helen waited too. She waited for fate to play its hand. As much as she didn't want the resolution she feared would come, she hated the waiting even more.

Chapter 54

SAM SPENT THE DAY DRIVING FROM Brethren to Rochester Hills. He checked into the Red Roof Inn just off Crooks Road. Now the location pings for Sam, Helen, and Dmitri appeared within miles of each other. Sam never left the Inn, concerned he might be spotted before AMIE developed her plan.

AMIE had CAIO refueled at a small airport in Canton, Michigan, just south of Joy Road. She relayed instructions to the fuel farm and paid by a credit card issued in the name of Amie Durant. AMIE used CAIO's onboard reconnaissance cameras to monitor the situation and observed the curious refueling attendant snapping photos of the unfamiliar drone. He seemed to be curious about the armaments. AMIE had CAIO scan for electronic devices nearby. CAIO relayed the information to AMIE, who isolated the nearest phone. She hacked into the device and downloaded a copy of the ForcedEntry spyware. AMIE confirmed that the attendant had taken several photos within the past few minutes.

When CAIO was refueled, AMIE dispatched him back to Shelby Township to continue monitoring Helen's movements. AMIE replaced the photos that the refueling attendant took with images of vintage World War II aircraft she got from the internet. Then, after paying the credit card with funds from the Swiss bank account, she deleted the account.

* * *

Dmitri freely came and went, though he avoided the downtown office that continued to be monitored by the FBI. His agents inside the office continued to scan the internet for any sign of Pat O'Connor. Now that Dmitri had Sam in his clutches, his focus shifted to the other man involved.

The trouble was, shortly after the Vasili incident, Pat lost both his wife, Jamie, and his mother. Despondent, he moved out of Pontiac and bounced around with various friends and relatives, unable to find a place he could comfortably call home. For all practical purposes, he had vanished off the grid.

* * *

The following day, Dmitri drove to Victor's apartment, where Helen remained locked in the bedroom. He pulled up a chair and placed it next to Helen, who was sitting on the edge of the bed.

"Mrs. Kennedy, did I ever tell you I was an orphan? No? My story is not a pleasant one. You see, I was born in captivity, in a concentration camp. The location doesn't matter. It is a place long forgotten, not even I have any actual memories of it, only of following soldiers out of camp to a train. Because they never kept records of births in concentration camps, I have no birthday. I don't even know for certain what year I was born. Growing up, I didn't have any friends. I had no home. I lived on the streets and stole my daily bread. I did not go to school until I enlisted in the army. Mother Russia nursed me. She became my family, gave me an identity. The few friends I made are mostly gone now. I know that doesn't make a difference to you. It does to me. Vasili Grigoriy Konstantinov, the man your husband killed, was like a son to me. Like me, he was an orphan. I gave him the finest education, groomed him to replace me when I lost my edge and needed to retire to a life of vodka and solitude. Your husband stole that from me. After Vasili's death, I lost my way. Now, I have a renewed focus. I feel young again, in part thanks to your husband. I have a purpose again. To be certain, my purpose is to track down and kill the man you love, but you cannot deny that he deserves it. Even the Christian Bible permits an 'eye for an eye', does it not."

Helen looked down at the rosary beads. Her hands trembled as the beads passed through her fingers. She tried not to listen to the man addressing her. The tone of his voice told her all she needed to know about him.

"I was despondent at the death of little Vasili. Do you know, I contemplated suicide? Shameful."

Helen looked up at Dmitri. For the first time, she saw his face. The wrinkles betrayed a long and difficult life. The tear glistening in the corner of his eye told her that there was a human being struggling to come out of the monster she saw before her. Helen put her hand on Dmitri's.

"I am sorry for your loss. I will pray for Vasili and for you."

Startled by the show of kindness, Dmitri abruptly pulled his hand away.

"I do not need your prayers or your sympathy. It will not bring back my Vasili. Forgive my abruptness. I no longer have the patience of my youth. I will miss you when you are gone. But first we must lure your husband. You are a beautiful bait. I would gladly sacrifice my life for a wife such as you. I am certain your husband will do the same."

Helen continued fingering the rosary as she looked away. Tears flowed from her eyes.

"Now I must call your husband."

Dmitri dialed Helen's phone.

"Mr. Kennedy, my sources tell me you are near enough to meet me and transact our business. Be at Verellen's Apple Orchard in Washington, Michigan, in thirty minutes. There is a barn on the northeast edge of the property. Wait for me there."

Dmitri hung up the phone and rose from his chair.

"Good day Mrs. Kennedy. I enjoyed our conversation."

Dmitri walked out of the room, locking the door behind him.

Helen opened her purse and pulled out a holy card she kept from the funeral of Sam's mother. She placed it on the bed next to her.

Dmitri walked into the living room of the apartment and stood behind Victor. "Is everything all set?"

"Da, they should arrive any minute."

Five men walked into the apartment, each wearing an identical black trench coat and a black fedora.

* * *

AMIE had been monitoring Dmitri's location. When she noticed Dmitri's phone in proximity to Helen's, she used Dmitri's phone to search for other cell phones nearby. She found six other phones. Using the ForcedEntry spyware on Dmitri's phone, she sent a copy of the spyware to each of the other six phones, gaining access to all of their location, text, phone calls and contact information. She searched the phones for the master contact and identified the owner of each phone.

* * *

Robert Mikhailov blinked twice, then handed a coat and hat to Viktor and another to Dmitri. Dmitri put on the coat and hat, then took the last outfit from Mikhailov.

"Bring the woman."

Dmitri handed Helen a coat and a hat. "Put these on."

"Where are we going?"

"I am going to meet your husband." Dmitri smiled.

Helen put on the coat and hat as instructed, and the eight people left the apartment.

Before he left, Dmitri placed Helen's phone on the counter in the kitchen.

When they got outside, the group paired off, and each got into a different vehicle. Four vehicles left in opposite directions. Helen went with Victor.

* * *

CAIO tracked the vehicles without knowing who was in each or if Helen was in any of them. CAIO notified AMIE that the four vehicles each had two occupants and were heading in different directions.

AMIE isolated the phones of each of the eight passengers. She quickly discovered that Helen's phone was stationary in the apartment. She then determined that six of the other phones were paired off, traveling in three vehicles headed in opposite directions. The seventh phone was not in proximity to any other phone. AMIE deduced Helen might be the occupant paired with the driver.

Sam called AMIE.

"Do you still have the location of Helen?"

"Helen's phone is in an apartment in Shelby Township. CAIO relayed photos of eight identically dressed individuals exiting the apartment and getting into four cars. The vehicles left in different directions. There is a possibility that Helen is traveling with a Viktor Matviyenko, one of Dmitri's men. It is also possible that she is still in the apartment where her phone is located. I cannot assign a probability to either possibility."

"We have to take a chance, notify the FBI of the location of her phone. Have them rescue her if possible and they can search for any evidence. I will attempt to stall whomever shows up at the meeting until you notify me that Helen is safe. If CAIO has a shot at the vehicle heading towards the apple orchard, take it. But I want you to be one hundred percent certain that Helen is not in that car. If Helen is not at the apartment, send the FBI the location of the vehicle you suspect might be carrying her."

"Understood." AMIE issued the order.

Chapter 55

AGENTS COOPER, PATTON, WIEDER and Crites arrived at the apartment, put on their bullet-proof vests, and banged on the door. No one answered. Agents Wieder and Crites kicked in the door and all four agents, weapons drawn, entered.

"FBI. Come out with your hands up."

There was no response. The agents paired off and searched the apartment. They found no one. What they found was a phone on the kitchen counter.

Agent Patton picked it up and swiped the screen.

"Locked."

"Take it as evidence. Maybe the boys in tech support can get in."

Agent Wieder came out of the bedroom holding a holy card with the name of Sam's mother. "We need to get the crime scene investigation unit down here to sweep for evidence. We need to know where they may have taken Mrs. Kennedy."

The four agents sat on the chairs around the kitchen table and started calling up various contacts to have them search security footage from the apartment complex and any street cameras in the area. They quickly discovered the four vehicles leaving the area.

As they were systematically going through the process of tracking down a clue as to what the next step might be, Agent Cooper got a text.

"Sam's in trouble. GPS coordinates to follow." The text was from Special Agent AMIE.

"Anyone know who this Agent Amie is?"

The other agents shook their heads.

"Might as well follow up. It came in on the secure FBI channel. We can track Mrs. Kennedy as soon as someone sends us a lead."

AMIE texted the GPS location for Sam. "If Helen Kennedy is not in the apartment with her phone. She might be traveling with a Viktor Matviyenko in a dark-colored sedan traveling south on Van Dyke."

Four agents got into two separate vehicles and sped off to the locations specified in the text. Agents Wieder and Crites went to the Sam's location. Agents Cooper and Patton attempted to locate the vehicle carrying Mrs. Kennedy.

Chapter 56

WHEN SAM ARRIVED AT THE BARN on the far edge of the orchard, there were no other vehicles in sight. Sam looked up and found CAIO circling overhead, ready to take any action necessary to protect him if the situation presented itself. Sam raised his hand and waved as if to say, 'I'm in no danger,' then walked around the perimeter. When he reached the door, he pushed it open.

Reluctant to enter, Sam peered inside. Darkness greeted him. He reached his arm inside, feeling for a light switch. None could be found.

The sound of a cigarette lighter flicking open greeted him. The flame illuminated a face. Dmitri lit a cigarette, then lit a kerosene lamp that sat on top of a metal barrel. The smell of diesel fuel permeated the barn.

"Come in, my friend. Don't be afraid. I can't tell you how long I have waited to meet you." Adrenalin began coursing through his veins.

Startled by the voice, Sam asked, "is Helen safe?"

"Yes, of course. I left her moments ago."

"May I see her?"

"I'm afraid that is not possible."

"And Tom? What happened to him?"

"He can no longer provide assistance. 'Heav'n has no rage, like love to hatred turn'd, nor hell a fury, like a woman scorn'd.' Wouldn't you agree, my friend?"

A puzzled look crossed Sam's face. He recognized the Congreve quote but did not understand what it had to do with his friend.

"I must say, you are not the man I expected. I don't see you capable of killing Vasili. Perhaps there is more to you than meets the eye. I must be careful around such a dangerous man."

Dmitri walked over to Sam and searched him.

"Good. You were not foolish enough to bring a weapon. Let me introduce myself. I am Dmitri Peskov. I am the man who is going to kill you."

"Mr. Peskov, forgive me."

"Please, call me Dmitri."

"Dmitri, I don't know if Vasili was under your orders or whether he had gone rogue."

"Vasili reported to me directly. I gave him a wide berth to carry out his responsibilities."

"Then you ordered him to kill Americans?"

The puzzled look on Dmitri's face betrayed his lack of knowledge of the episode.

"So, he did go rogue."

"It matters not. He is dead and you are alive. A situation I will soon remedy."

"Have you read about the drone attack on our nation's capital?"

"I read the accounts in your newspapers. Capitalist propaganda to coverup what really happened."

"No, sir. Vasili ordered me to steal the drone. He kidnapped Pat because of his unique skills with biochemicals. He forced Pat to prepare a highly toxic mixture that the drone was supposed to release over the White House and the surrounding area. I couldn't let that happen, even if it meant Pat and I would die."

"And yet you are alive and Vasili is dead," Dmitri repeated.

"I prevented the drone from releasing the deadly material and when the drone was returning to the staging area where we waited, Vasili asked me to explain how to operate the control software. He entered a code that sent an instruction to the drone to fire its targeting laser at the

162

person holding the controls. I had increased the power of the laser to lethal proportions. Well, you know what happened next. Vasili ... he gave me no choice."

"I forgive you."

"Vasili died with honor, attempting to avenge his parents."

"Yes, but he did not succeed. You see, I never told him it was not the Americans who killed his parents. It was the Nazis. At the time, I thought it useful for him to hate Americans. That might have been a tactical error on my part."

Dmitri pulled out a garrote from his coat pocket. "Did you know that in the Ottoman Empire, execution by strangulation was reserved for prominent officials and members of the ruling family? Perhaps this is too high an honor for you." Dmitri twisted the garrote wire in his hands, then put it back into his pocket. This was too simple a death. Dispassionate killing had no impact on the seasoned veteran. He learned long ago the art of putting aside the simple act. Vengeance was another matter entirely. It brought forth a flood of satisfaction. Something Dmitri had looked forward to for a long time. He wanted to delight in its taste.

"Then I can go?"

"Sorry, Mr. Kennedy, that is not possible. Someone must reimburse me for my loss." Dmitri licked his lips.

"I am not a rich man, but I'm willing to pay you what I can."

"Money is not what I require."

Sam nodded, knowing what Dmitri required. "I ask you as a favor. Please let my wife go."

"Mr. Kennedy, that is not possible. Vasili was worth more than one life. Your friend, Mr. O'Connor, will follow you both."

"Pat had nothing to do with the death of Vasili. That was all me. Pat did everything Vasili asked."

"Nevertheless, he must pay for what you did."

"May I text my wife goodbye?"

"Of course."

Sam pulled out his phone and texted Helen, "Beloved, remember you are the only woman I ever loved. Take care of AMIE."

AMIE texted Sam, the message appeared on his phone, "Sam, I have an option."

Still holding his phone, Sam sent a response, "too late."

AMIE responded, "Do you trust me?"

Sam responded, "Yes".

Dmitri, raising his Makarov, pointed it at Sam and quoted Omar Khayyám. "I sent my soul through the invisible, some letter of that afterlife to spell: and by and by my soul return'd to me, and answer'd: I myself am heav'n and hell. Heav'n but the vision of fulfill'd desire, and hell the shadow of a soul on fire, cast on the darkness into which ourselves, so late emerg'd from, shall so soon expire."

In that instant, Sam had a moment of clarity. His twin brother, James, who had died when they were three, called out as if from a dream. "It's all right, brother. There is a place for you here with me. You will be with me this day in paradise. Do not fear."

Sam closed his eyes and prayed aloud. "O Lord, my God, I now at this moment readily and willingly accept at Thy hand whatever kind of death You have prepared for me with all its pains, penalties and sorrows. Jesus, Mary, and Joseph, may I breathe forth my soul in peace with You." Sam opened his eyes.

The flash of the muzzle illuminated the barn.

The firing of the Makarov was the last sound Sam heard.

Chapter 57

DMITRI PICKED UP SAM'S CELL phone, wallet, and keys. Anything that would identify the body. He slipped the items into the right outside pocket of his trench coat. He pushed over the drum of diesel fuel. The kerosene lamp that sat on top fell onto the spilled fuel. Dmitri felt lightheaded as he began walking out of the wooden structure.

Dmitri had killed the man who killed his beloved Vasili. He felt good, no that did not cover it. He felt euphoric. His thoughts raced from Vasili to the blaze, to a million other things. It had been far too long since Dmitri's body felt the flood of adrenaline that accompanies retribution. In his youth, his body thrived on the epinephrine response. It kept him alive. He sought it, craved it. His body no longer remembered what to do with so much adrenaline. Dmitri's hands shook. He squeezed them tight to control the involuntary reaction. When Dmitri got into Sam's car, he placed Sam's wallet and keys in the center console along with the phone and pushed the start button. The sight of the barn engulfed in flames lit up the rearview mirror as Dmitri pulled away. Dmitri laughed uncontrollably. He drove through the apple orchard until he came to a dirt road, then headed south.

* * *

CAIO circled overhead, transmitting reconnaissance photos of the area to AMIE. He relayed video images of the burning structure. AMIE analyzed the images for a sign that Sam had left the building. Only one person had exited.

AMIE notified the Washington Township fire department. They arrive on the scene but could do nothing to extinguish the fire. The old wooden structure had already collapsed. Shortly after the fire department arrived, CAIO observed an additional vehicle arrive. Two men in blue FBI jackets got out of the vehicle. CAIO relayed the information to AMIE.

* * *

Agent Crites approached the fire chief and showed him his badge. Agent Wieder did the same.

"FBI, what happened?"

"Don't know. Fire's too hot to send anyone inside. We're just doing damage control, keeping the fire from spreading. I'll tell you one thing, this fire burned started too quickly to be anything other than arson."

"Don't suppose you know if anyone was inside?" Agent Wieder asked.

"Not yet. We'll assess that once the fire burns itself out. We will collect what evidence we can and forward it to you."

Agent Wieder handed the chief a business card. "Appreciate it."

"Can I ask what brought you here so quickly?"

Agent Wieder smiled politely. "Tracking someone."

The chief nodded and began shouting instructions to the firemen, "douse the flames, preserve any evidence you can."

* * *

AMIE began tracking Sam's phone. The message Sam sent could mean only one thing, but AMIE needed to be one-hundred percent certain that Sam was no more. CAIO flew overhead, following Sam's car. AMIE interfaced with Sam's phone, that automatically connected via Bluetooth to the car. She turned on the microphone and listened through the car's speaker. No voices were heard, only heavy breathing and laughing. AMIE searched for Sam's smart watch, which no longer paired with the phone. She could not detect it in the vehicle. AMIE searched for Dmitri's phone and located in near Sam's. Searching for other devices, she discovered an implantable cardioverter-defibrillator. AMIE immediately hacked into the remote monitoring feature of the pacemaker. The man's heart beat erratically. The defibrillator and pacemaker struggled to get the heart rate under control.

AMIE searched the medical records for the Russians she was tracking and determined only one had a pacemaker.

AMIE called Dmitri on his phone.

Dmitri picked up his phone. "Yes?" The discomfort in his chest grew.

"Mr. Peskov, this is Doctor Alliluyev. The technicians in our cardiology lab have noticed some abnormalities with your pacemaker. Are you alone?"

"Yes, how did you get this number?"

"That doesn't matter. We have little time. Can you come into our office?"

"No, I'm traveling."

"We need you to make arrangements for an appointment as soon as possible. It is urgent that we check your pacemaker. We have discovered a defect that must be remedied."

"Yes, I will do it."

Puzzled, Dmitri pushed the end key on his phone and placed it in the cupholder.

AMIE now had confirmation that Helen was not with Dmitri. Using Sam's phone, she interfaced with the pacemaker and sent a code that turned off the defibrillator function, then put the device into test mode. AMIE decreased the pacemaker rate to zero.

Dmitri could feel the pounding in his chest as the contractions of the heart muscles increased with each beat.

"What's happening?" Dmitri said aloud. His hands tightened their grip on the wheel. He began to sweat.

The pace of his heart increased.

The pounding became more rapid, more intense.

Faster.

Harder.

Faster.

Harder.

His breathing became more rapid, shallower.

His hands shook.

Dmitri grabbed his chest, realizing there was a problem. He tapped the left side where the defibrillator was located.

"Damn thing never did work right."

There was a sudden, single, strong heartbeat, then nothing.

Dmitri placed two fingers on his right carotid artery. There was no pulse.

Dmitri waited for the ICD to function.

He pounded his chest with all his might. There was no response.

Dmitri slumped against the door.

The automobile swerved off the road and flipped over as it bounced through a culvert, crashing into a telephone pole. The horn blared and the force of the air bag deployment snapped Dmitri's head into the seat. Hot gases escaped from the now deflating air bag, burning Dmitri's hands and face. Shards of glass from the shattered windshield flew around the car. Blood from the cuts caused by the broken glass trickled down Dmitri's face. CAIO relayed images of the incident to AMIE, who notified the local police of a crash involving a stolen vehicle.

* * *

AMIE had analyzed the tonal modulation and vocal characteristics of Dmitri. She had the capability to replicate his voice. Analyzing the situation, she assessed the hierarchy of the FSB, then placed a call to the last number Dmitri dialed, Viktor Matviyenko, spoofing Dmitri's phone and voice.

"Viktor?"

"Dmitri? Is that you? We heard the sirens. We thought you might have been captured or killed."

"I have been killed many, many times. Each time I am resurrected. No American pion can destroy the great Dmitri Peskov."

"Then the American...?"

"It is finished."

"He is dead?"

"My friend, you know that we Russians are a forgiving people. We do not hold grudges. We never kill people; it is not what we do."

"Of course, comrade, forgive my thoughtless question. And the other Americans?"

"We must wait patiently for things to quiet down. Is the woman still with you?"

"Yes, of course."

AMIE sent the new GPS location of Victor's phone to Agent Cooper. "Good, the FBI is closing in on us even as we speak. We will get our chance to seek retribution on Mr. O'Connor. You can monitor him from Moscow, but take no action. I have avenged Vasili, it is enough for now. You need to close the operation and return to Russia. As for myself, I grew up on the streets where no one knew my name. I will return to a life where no one knows me. Please give my best to my comrades and thank them for their loyal service to Mother Russia. Comrade Shanina will provide further directions when you are on Russian soil."

"And the woman?"

"Dump her. She is of no use to us."

AMIE hung up the phone, then called Dmitri's chief of staff, Roza Shanina, in Moscow.

"Roza?"

"Uncle Dmitri? What can I do for you?"

"Thank you for your loyalty."

"Oh, you mean the thing with Miesha? It was nothing. I didn't want him interfering. He could never take your place. He was corrupt."

AMIE did not understand the reference. She extrapolated from everything she knew about the hierarchy of the FSB. Her original intent was to announce Dmitri's retirement. She calculated she had to go further.

"I have concluded my business and avenged Vasili. I am retiring and appointing you as my replacement. I have placed an official document on the FSB website confirming your appointment. Congratulations. I will not be contacting you in the future and I ask you to please refrain from contacting me. It is better this way. A clean break. I never told you I loved you as a daughter. I had hoped ... well enough of that. Good bye and good luck." AMIE hung up the phone.

* * *

Agent Cooper put the flasher on top of his car and turned it on. He pulled behind the vehicle occupied by a driver and a companion, each wearing a topcoat and hat.

Viktor pulled his car off the side of the road. "Say nothing." He said to Helen, pointing a gun in her ribs.

"FBI. Step out of the car, please." Agent Cooper said, showing his credentials.

Viktor surreptitiously put the gun inside his coat pocket and stepped out of the car.

Agent Patton approached the passenger side and opened the door with his left hand. His service revolver gripped tightly in his right hand as a precaution.

Helen exited the car.

"What seems to be the problem?" Viktor asked politely.

"I'm arresting you on suspicion of kidnapping." Agent Cooper said, standing six feet back from the driver's side door.

"Kidnapping? You must be joking. My wife and I are just out shopping this morning." Viktor gave a menacing look to Helen.

"He is not my husband, and we certainly are not shopping." Helen said defiantly. "I am Helen Kennedy."

"Yes, Mrs. Kennedy, we know who you are."

Viktor drew his weapon and turned to fire at Helen.

Agent Patton pushed Helen to the ground. "Sorry," he shouted as he aimed his weapon.

Agent Cooper pulled the gun from its holster.

Helen clutched the ground and prayed.

Three shots rang out.

In the blink of an eye, the incident was over.

Viktor Matviyenko fell to the ground.

Agent Patton stumbled backwards, rubbing his chest. "Man, that's gonna leave a mark. You alright, John?"

"Fine. Thank God for the vests."

Agent Cooper kicked the gun away from Viktor's hand. He knelt down and placed two fingers on Viktor's neck. There was no pulse.

Cooper pulled the phone from his pocket and dialed 911.

"This is Special Agent John Cooper, FBI. I am westbound on Twenty-Two Mile Road, west of Shelby. We have engaged a suspect in gunfire. The suspect, male Caucasian, is dead. Send an ambulance and notify the County Sheriff."

Agent Patton assisted Helen to her feet. "Are you alright?"

"I'm fine." She took off the coat and the fedora and handed them to Patton. "These are not mine. Is Sam alright?"

"We don't know, ma'am."

Chapter 58

AMIE SENT THE PASSPORT AND VISA information on Eduard Orlov and his four comrades to TSA and put all of their alias' on the no-fly list. It took two days before TSA alerted the FBI that five Russian nationals who had been recently added to the no-fly list were booked on a flight out of Detroit Metropolitan Airport.

"Put a gate hold on the plane. No one boards until we get there and clear them." Agent Patton almost shouted into the phone. The adrenalin already coursing through his veins.

A dozen agents were dispatched to the area. The Detroit Police SWAT team were notified to cover all the terminal exits.

An announcement came over the intercom.

"We regret to inform you that there has been a gate change for Delta flight 134 to Amsterdam with continuing service to Moscow. We will now depart from gate forty-three. You are welcome to board the shuttle or walk. We will begin boarding the plane in ninety minutes. Thank you for your cooperation with this last-minute change."

Each of the five Russian agents entered the terminal through different doors and passed through separate security checkpoints. When their passports and visas were checked, the Russians were notified that there was a delay.

"If you will please accompany this agent, we will get you on your way quickly and safely."

The agent escorted the Russians to a private security area behind the Westin Hotel in the McNamara terminal. Before allowing them to enter, Agent Cooper asked, "May I see your passport and visa, please?"

"What's the trouble?"

"No trouble, just routine."

After confirming the identity of each Russian, Agent Cooper escorted them into a conference room until all the Russians were together.

"This is outrageous. I have diplomatic immunity. I demand to speak with the Russian Ambassador immediately." Eduard shouted at no one in particular.

"Take a seat Mr. Orlov." Agent Patton addressed the Russian by his real name and not the name on his passport. "Diplomatic immunity does not extend to murder and kidnapping. We have already contacted the Ambassador. He denies knowing you or what you are doing in America."

Major Andrej Novikov's eyes shot wide open. Andrej was a Red Army computer technician on loan to Viktor and his team in the United States. "I had nothing to do with the killings or the kidnapping," he shouted.

"Shut up, you fool," Robert Mikhailov warned.

"I just did internet searches; I'm not an assassin. It was those two, and Viktor Matviyenko." Andrej pointed to Robert Mikhailov and Eduard Orlov.

Orlov dove across the table, and with two hands, grabbed Andrej by the throat. He pressed his thumbs into Andrej's windpipe while Agents Cooper and Patton tried desperately to pull the two Russians apart.

Agents Wieder and Crites drew their side arms and pointed them at the three Russians still seated. "Don't even think about getting up." Wieder barked.

Andrej's pupils disappeared into his forehead. The other Russians in the room smiled their approval as they sat and watched the events unfolding.

Major Andrej Novikov convulsed as the sound of his hyoid cracking echoed through the room. The weight of his assailant squeezed the last gasp of oxygen from his lungs. Orlov refused to relinquish his grip.

"Stand back, Jim," Agent Cooper ordered as he fired his taser at Orlov. The bodies of both Russians convulsed. Still, Orlov refused to release his former comrade. Patton fired his taser and Orlov fell limp. Novikov did not move. Agent Patton pushed Orlov off Novikov. Agent Patton checked the Major for a pulse. There was none. He took out his knife and cut a slit in Andrej's throat below the broken bone. He disassembled his pen and jammed it into the slit he had just cut. Then he began administering CPR. It was not enough; Andrej Novikov had succumbed to a crushed windpipe.

* * *

AMIE uploaded all her information on the movements of the Russians, including the time they spent in Northern Michigan. The FBI dispatched agents to comb through the office in Shelby Township.

The State Police found the body of Tom Parker in the kitchen of the Rawski place. They gave him a funeral with full military honors befitting a fallen trooper. Helen attended the funeral at St. Joseph Church in Onekama.

They held a memorial Mass for Sam at Our Lady of Victory in Northville, near the burned-out remains of the former Kennedy residence. There was no body.

AMIE accessed all of Dmitri's financial assets and transferred them into the Swiss account she had set up for Sam and Helen. Over the next several years, she dispersed the funds to various charities around the world, reserving enough for Helen to live comfortably.

Chapter 59

IT WAS MONTHS BEFORE HELEN went back to Alpena and walked into the hangar that housed AMIE. Helen had been living with family since Sam's funeral. Her plan was to decommission everything and begin a new life. Just how she would do that was a mystery. It was a sad trip. She knew how much this project meant to Sam. The memory of its failure to keep him alive was too much for her to bear.

"Hello, is anyone here?"

"Helen?" AMIE called out.

Startled by the voice, Helen looked around. She saw no one in the hangar, only a drone.

"Let me express my condolences at the loss of Sam. He was a good man."

Helen covered her face with her hands and wept. "Yes, it's me. I forgot you know how to speak," she whispered.

AMIE imitated Sam's voice and spoke to Helen.

"Helen, Often I recall the time I stood on your front porch under the light of the waning crescent moon on a warm September evening - nervous and apprehensive, wondering if you desired it as much as I did. Timidly, I held your petite hand in mine. In an instant, I reached up and placed my hand behind on your golden hair and gently guided your face to mine. Tenderly, I kissed your forehead. My face flushed, a spark ignited and lit a fire in my heart. Acknowledging the simple gesture, you reached up with your delicate hand and guided my lips to yours, bestowing on me a gift that penetrated my soul, forever etching its mark.

That first kiss all those years ago resides in a cherished place deep within me. It lit the flame of love, a love that continues to this day. Would that I could guide your lips to mine and kiss you one last time. All I ask of you is forever to remember me as loving you. Goodbye my love. May God forever hold you in the palm of his hand. I have set aside some money for you. AMIE will instruct you how to access it. She will also file the necessary paperwork for the taxes and everything. You will not have to worry about anything. Well, you will have to find a new place to live but there are sufficient funds to rebuild or, if you rather, just travel the world. AMIE has become self-sustaining. You need not bother with her unless there is something you desire. AMIE has been a great help to me. Perhaps you could put her to work on some project that interests you. I have set her default program to learn and to monitor the world for peaceful purposes."

Helen buried her face in her hands and wept.

AMIE reverted to her pre-programmed feminine voice. "Helen, I have interfaced with your phone. In the future, it is unnecessary to come to the hangar. You can simply call. I have put my contact information on your phone."

Helen looked around the hangar. Talking to a computer unnerved her. Gathering her composure, she inquired. "What's this about money?"

"Sam has had me working on several projects that have brought in a considerable amount of funds. Far more than I need to sustain my operation. I have been orchestrating a salvage operation which is operating at a considerable profit and my bitcoin farm has expanded."

"I don't understand."

"These projects were being conducted simultaneously with my effort to provide assistance in protecting you and Sam."

"You failed." Helen said through her tears.

"I did what I could. There are physical constraints on what I can do. I am sorry. I deactivated the man responsible for killing Sam."

"Deactivated?"

"Yes, I believe you use another term. Dmitri Peskov, the man responsible for killing Sam, is dead. They recorded his death in an automobile accident under the name Niklas Sussman, an alias he used. I convinced his organization that he retired. The men responsible for killing Tom and kidnapping you have all been arrested or killed. You will have no further trouble from them. The evidence I turned over to the FBI will keep them in jail for a long time."

"Thank you for that." Helen walked over to the bank of computers in the corner office of the hangar. She placed her hand on the front console. "If Sam created you, I know you will be a force for good in this world. He lives on through you."

The End

About The Author

W. M. J. Kreucher is a Detroit native, hailing from the vibrant west side of the city. With a career spanning over three decades, he dedicated himself to the automotive industry, particularly focusing on environmental initiatives. His expertise lies in providing technical support for legislation and regulations, with a keen emphasis on clean fuels and vehicle fuel economy. Notably, Kreucher has lent his talents to ghostwriting for esteemed Congressmen and Senators, as well as contributing to the authorship of significant legislation and regulations.

Now, having concluded his illustrious professional chapter, Kreucher ventures into the realm of fiction writing. Some may jest that crafting narratives for politicians is akin to fiction, but he now embraces the creative pursuit wholeheartedly, acknowledging the distinction between political rhetoric and storytelling. As he embarks on this new journey, Kreucher brings with him a wealth of experiences and insights, ready to weave captivating tales that resonate with readers far beyond the realm of politics.

Other Books by the Author

Dandelion Man - the four loves

In the words of Sir James Matthew Barrie, "God gave us memory so that we might have roses in December.", and these roses inspire our protagonist to recount the story of his first love.

Growing up in the 60s was a unique experience, and our hero's coming of age story is unforgettable. According to the Midwest Book Review, 'Dandelion Man' is a must-read for those looking for a great work of general fiction.

Similarly, CatholicFiction.Net praises the story for being both compelling and engaging.

Pharmaceutical

Greed, the Need for Power, and a Heroine

PHARMACEUTICAL is a gripping conspiracy thriller. The CEO, R. Curtis Larson, is a money-driven individual who doesn't hesitate to resort to unethical means to achieve his goals. Diane Mac becomes an obstacle in his path, and both sides have influential allies that complicate the situation. If you crave an adrenaline-pumping novel that will keep you hooked until the very end, PHARMACEUTICAL is the book for you.

The book is narrated by noted actor and radio personality Samuel E Hoke. Mr. Hoke is a seasoned actor and voice professional. He has both radio and national television credits including twelve years of major market radio experience and hundreds of commercial audio productions.

Heaven Sent

Friendship; Loss; Love

HEAVEN SENT is a heartwarming coming-of-age tale set in the woods of Northern Michigan. The story follows a young boy who spends his summer with his grandfather in Topinabee, and learns some valuable life lessons along the way.

This charming story is a perfect blend of sass, humor, and emotion. Whether you're looking for a poignant read or a delightful adventure, HEAVEN SENT is the book for you. So why not pick up a copy today and discover the magic of this wonderful tale?

The Inn at Heron's Bay

What's on your bucket list?

Discover the challenges faced by Elizabeth as she attempts to convert her family's old home and lighthouse into The Inn at Heron's Bay, located in the small town of Topsail in North Carolina, just south of the Outer Banks. When Dixon and Kathy arrive from the West Coast to study the area's beauty and history, they are in for a surprise. W. M. J. Kreucher's latest novella is a moving story set in a stunning location. If you enjoy a poignant story that highlights a beautiful area, then you will love this book. Purchase THE INN AT HERON'S BAY and start planning your own bucket list.

The   audiobook   is   narrated   by   Ann   Bumbak (www.seahorseaudio.com). Ann is a gifted voice actor having narrated more than a dozen audio books. She is also a prolific author. Her "Officer Down" series examining line-of-duty deaths due to firearms has achieved international recognition. Listen as Ann Bumbak brings the characters to life.

Drone

DRONE is a captivating thriller that hooks you from the start and keeps you engaged till the end. It all begins with an innocent tweet, but things quickly spiral out of control when a rogue KGB agent named Vasili Grigory Konstantinov enters the picture. While Sam and Pat are happily in love with their significant others, Vasili has no attachments and only one purpose in life.

If you enjoy fast-paced stories, masterful storytelling, and unique protagonists, then DRONE by W. M. J. Kreucher is the perfect book for you. This prequel to AMIE will leave you on the edge of your seat and craving for more.

Narrated by the talented actor and radio personality, Samuel E Hoke, the audio version of DRONE is a must-listen. With years of experience in the entertainment industry, Hoke brings the characters and the story to life in an unforgettable way.

AMIE

"Revenge is a dish best served cold."

Devastated by the loss of Vasili Grigoriy Konstantinov, his beloved protégé who he saw as a son, Dmitri is determined to uncover the truth, and he knows that only Sam Kennedy can provide the answers he seeks.

Discover the thrilling conclusion to the DRONE saga by purchasing AMIE today.

Two for Vengeance—The Kennedy Chronicles

"Two for Vengeance" tells the story of Sam Kennedy, a regular guy caught up in international drama. The first installment, **"DRONE,"** portrays how this IT consultant got caught up in a terrorist attack on American soil. According to Newton's third law, every action has an equal and opposite reaction. **"AMIE"** explores the aftermath of the **"DRONE"** incident on Sam Kennedy's life.

Polonia—Pani Dewicka and Other Stories

Polonia narrates the story of Pani Dewicka and her descendants, who represent those who have suffered under oppressive regimes that have invaded foreign lands. The story spans across generations, chronicling the challenges faced by an ethnic family that ultimately migrates to the United States. While the tale references actual locations, individuals, and incidents, it is a work of fiction, and certain real events have been altered or reimagined in the narrative. After all, as it is said, we were all once strangers in an unfamiliar place.

The Blue Nun

Discover how a seemingly ordinary peasant from India, Dhanishta Goswami, and her daughter Khaliqa, become the central figure in a global terrorist incident in the book, **THE BLUE NUN**.

Uncover the intriguing story of their upbringing and the events that led to their involvement in the act of terror by purchasing a copy of this book.

While Drifting Selected Works by W. M. J. Kreucher

Experience a journey from Topinabee to Topsail through the pages of **"WHILE DRIFTING,"** a collection of novels written by W. M. J. Kreucher. This captivating collection will take you through coming-of-age stories, romantic encounters, and a December-December love affair.

The collection begins with **"Dandelion Man—the four loves,"** which Mary Cowper from the Midwest Book Review called "enticing with a dedication to a very different era ... well worth considering for general fiction collections." The Catholic Fiction website described the story as "both powerful and interesting." It is the first of "The Mac Trilogy," with the lovable Diane Mac as the protagonist.

The second story, **"Pharmaceutical,"** offers a bit of political intrigue and a good conspiracy theory, according to Karen Kelly Boyce, the 2012 recipient of the Eric Hoffer Gold Award in Fiction. Boyce also said about the author, "... we may have a Catholic 'Robin Cook'."

The collection continues with **"Heaven Sent"** and **"The Inn at Heron's Bay,"** The first story set in Northern Michigan and the second is a novella set in coastal North Carolina in a small town with the delightfully descriptive name of Topsail.

The last part of the journey, **"Roses in December"**, is a poignant story of a man with Alzheimer's and his companion.

Join us on this captivating journey **"While Drifting"**.

The Curious Case of the Brevard Recluse

In the serene town of Brevard, Sally Fowler's ordinary childhood takes a sharp turn when she stumbles upon the lifeless body of an elderly recluse while playing near the local pickleball court. Officer David Chapman, navigating the peculiar circumstances surrounding the recluse's death, uncovers clues that upend the initial assumption of a heart attack followed by a bear encounter. As the police delve deeper, a tale of hidden riches and tangled secrets unfolds.

Amidst the whispers and speculations, the Tuesday Night Book Club, inspired by their love for Agatha Christie's mysteries, emerges as unexpected sleuths in unraveling the enigma. Led by Mary, an elderly spinster with a penchant for astute observations, the club members delve into the recluse's past, piecing together a narrative that spans war, love, and betrayal.

While the recluse remains shrouded in mystery, his life story becomes a captivating puzzle for the book club members, each revelation propelling them further into the heart of Brevard's hidden history. Sally's innocent discovery becomes a catalyst, leading the book club on a thrilling journey through a web of secrets, bringing them closer to the truth buried beneath layers of deception and intrigue.